A Convincing Arrangement with a Brute

A Clean Regency Romance Novel

Martha Barwood

Copyright © 2024 by Martha Barwood
All Rights Reserved.
This book may not be reproduced or transmitted in any form without the written permission of the publisher. In no way is it legal to reproduce, duplicate, or transmit any part of this document in either electronic means or in printed format. Recording of this publication is strictly prohibited and any storage of this document is not allowed unless with written permission from the publisher.

Austin Thomas
Lavender Latrice

Table of Contents

Prologue 4
Chapter One 7
Chapter Two 13
Chapter Three 17
Chapter Four 21
Chapter Five 27
Chapter Six 33
Chapter Seven 41
Chapter Eight 46
Chapter Nine 50
Chapter Ten 59
Chapter Eleven 66
Chapter Twelve 72
Chapter Thirteen 80
Chapter Fourteen 87
Chapter Fifteen 95
Chapter Sixteen 103
Chapter Seventeen 111
Chapter Eighteen 122
Chapter Nineteen 129
Chapter Twenty 135
Chapter Twenty-One 143
Chapter Twenty-Two 151
Chapter Twenty-Three 157

Chapter Twenty-Four 162
Chapter Twenty-Five 166
Epilogue..174
Extended Epilogue 182

Prologue

He had to be in the wrong place.

Noise assaulted his ears until his hands itched with the urge to cup them. Vincent Latrice was quite used to hustle and bustle, accustomed to loud and abrasive men shouting at him to get their businesses done. In his line of work, Vincent assumed that he had interacted with all walks of life. But this? This was unlike anything he had seen before and he wanted to leave.

Only the single sheet of paper in his hand kept him where he was as he stared at the sight before him. Roars erupted into the night sky, which was oddly devoid of light. It seemed both the moon and the stars were hiding from the violent scene below. Only a few paces away from him, two men grappled with each other, one of the men putting the other in a headlock. Onlookers shouted their encouragements, while others stood off to the side placing their bets.

He was at a fighting ring.

Not just any fighting ring, though. The likes of which were often whispered in hush tones among men, the outcomes talked about for days until the next. Vincent couldn't believe that it was happening at the very same dock he would accept shipment of his goods.

With a quiet sigh, he looked down at the hastily written contract he'd done just before leaving his comfortable manor to come to...this place. The terms were simple, he thought. Yet weighty enough that he wasn't sure if the other party would be willing to sign.

Vincent looked up when the crowd roared again. One of the men was struggling to get to his feet while the other stood over him with his fists raised. Vincent's eyes remained on the man standing. He wasn't nearly as bloody and bruised as his opponent and the size difference between them marked him as the clear winner before the match even began. Those who had placed their bets on the man still attempting to stand shouted lewd things at him, their frustration obvious.

A burly man stepped into the ring just as the struggling fighter collapsed. The crowd erupted, the noise so deafening that it was a wonder they weren't disrupting the nearby neighborhood. Vincent couldn't even hear the victor being announced.

He studied the man's face. He didn't smile, didn't even seem to care that he had won his fight. He just sauntered out of the ring, in Vincent's direction.

"My lord." Vincent stepped in his path. The man's eyes flashed with irritation before his entire expression curled with it.

"Do not call me that here," he hissed. Then he looked Vincent up and down. "Who are you?"

"Should I call you by your given name then?" Vincent asked. All he received were narrowed eyes in response. "Austin then. I have been looking for you."

Austin didn't deign to reply. He crossed his arms and waited.

Vincent ignored the tickle of apprehension at the base of his spine. He'd dealt with more dangerous men than him, he reminded himself. Then again, there weren't many bastards who could say they'd claimed an earldom. Austin Thomas might be more dangerous than Vincent gave him credit for.

"A friend of mine—and I suppose of yours as well—told me where I could find you," Vincent explained. "I have a proposition for you."

"I am not interested."

Austin attempted to walk away but Vincent caught his shoulder. At the look Austin gave him, he quickly let go. "It will be worth your while, I assure you. I have done my research and I know you are in need of money, which I have. All you have to do is—"

"I said, I am not interested." The ice in his voice could have frozen a volcano but Vincent would not be deterred. Austin was his only hope. If he didn't want to take him up on his offer, then his sister was doomed.

"Read it first." Boldly, Vincent shoved the crumpled contract into Austin's hand and quickly backed away. "My address is stated on that paper. If you would like to take me up on the offer then visit me. If not, you may ignore it."

"I said I don—"

"Thank you!" Vincent turned and jogged off, not daring to look back. He listened for footsteps behind him and only breathed a sigh of relief when he realized that he wasn't being followed.

That didn't mean he was going to accept his offer, however. Vincent understood that but he didn't dare to consider the possibility. He couldn't. His sister's future was riding on Austin's acceptance. Or else she would die a spinster.

Chapter One

Becoming the Earl of Derby might have been a terrible mistake.

Austin was willing to blame the earldom for his current situation and not his refusal to accept what came with it. Dismissing his coachman earlier had sounded like a fine idea at first. He didn't need someone carrying him around. He'd done well without that luxury before so he had no need for it now.

But with every grueling step he took, he was beginning to wonder if he might have been a little hasty in his dismissal. The sun beat down on him as if it aimed to make him regret what he'd done, sweat running down the back of his neck. The contract he'd tucked into his waistcoat seemed to burn right through his skin. At this point, he wondered if he should just turn around.

Walking would do him some good, he told himself. The megrim pounding in the base of his skull made his eyesight a little splotchy, but at least the fresh air helped a little. And he needed to think about what he was about to do. Needed additional time to back out of his decision.

Still, he pressed on. He had no choice, he thought bitterly. This was the only option he had left.

Latrice Manor came into view the moment he rounded the corner. It was an ornate slab of white brick, taller than the others and sporting a sizeable front yard behind its iron-wrought gate. Opulence dripped from every inch of the manor. Austin gritted his teeth.

This is a mistake, he thought as he headed for the manor. *I should turn around right now.*

He kept going, even though every bone in his body urged him not to. These were the kind of people he despised. He was about to walk into the home of a rich man who thought he owned the world just because he was deemed upper class.

But would a rich man approach him late at night, at a fighting ring, and all but beg him to sign a contract? A contract that basically sold his sister into marriage?

The poor woman had to be a sorry sight if this was what they had to resort to.

Austin knew he was no better. He might be deemed handsome if he ever cared to wear a more pleasant expression but it was not his lack of physical appeal that rendered him ineligible for matrimony. It was his true status as a bastard. He wouldn't have cared if it hadn't been for the fact that, in the position he stood in now, he *had* to get married.

Even their front gate was overdone. Latrice Manor was interwoven in the metal, the gate so tall that even Austin would not have been able to touch the top without jumping. He stood and stared for a moment, the name giving him pause. It nagged at him since last night, as if he should know it.

And then it hit him. He knew the name Latrice. A man without title but with enough wealth to put him in rooms with earls and dukes. He'd even gotten an audience with the Prince Regent himself. Dubbed the Merchant of Brentwood, the Latrice family sat atop a shipping empire.

A mistake, he thought again as he pushed the gate open and approached the front door. He used the obnoxiously large knocker on the door and listened to the sound echo on the other side.

Only a few seconds later, the door opened to reveal a thin-lipped butler with spectacles perched on the very tip of his nose. The butler slid the spectacles just a bit further down to look Austin up and down.

"May I help you?" he asked, his slow drawl so haughty that Austin curled his hands into fists on instinct.

He swallowed the irritation he felt at the butler's tone and pushed through gritted teeth, "I am here to see the master of this house."

"Mr. Latrice is not available at the moment." The butler raised his chin, clasping his hands behind him. "What is your name, sir?"

Austin nearly curled his upper lip in annoyance. He thought such a disdainful demeanor was only reserved for the upper class. "None of your business," Austin replied. "Now step aside. I do not have time to waste here."

"Sir." The butler stepped in Austin's path, stopping him from crossing over the threshold. It looked as if he was trying his best to hold back his own annoyance. "I understand that you may be eager to learn under Mr. Latrice's expertise but as I have stated before, he is busy. So he is not available to attend to you at the moment. So if you could please leave—"

"I am the Earl of Derby," Austin snapped. "And your Mr. Latrice is expecting me. Now step out of the way or else I will remove you myself. And I don't think you will fancy me doing that."

Horror flashed across the butler's face for a split second before he masked it quickly. He took a discreet step backward, clearing his throat. It took everything in Austin not to shove the man aside when he gave him another once-over, as if he was deciding whether or not he should believe him.

His clothes weren't very fashionable, Austin knew. And the lengthy walk from his townhouse had covered his waistcoat and breeches in a fine layer of dust. So yes, he may not look like a proper earl right now and usually, Austin wouldn't care about that. But if this butler insisted on standing in his way—and if Austin wanted to keep this civil—then throwing his title in the butler's face was the only way to get past this door, as much as he hated to do it.

For a moment, he thought he would really have to resort to a less favorable option but then the butler said, "Forgive me, my lord. Please, follow me."

Stiffly, he turned and walked away. Austin grunted in annoyance and followed behind him. He should just turn around. Everything in him was telling him that this was a bad idea, even if it sounded good on paper. Nothing good would come from involving himself with these people and this odd contract.

But he needed the funds. For his father. For his late stepmother. And for the legacy they left behind.

"But, Vincent, you promised!"

The shrill voice nearly made Austin stop in his tracks. The butler was slowing down and then he halted in front of a door that was slightly ajar. Instead of indicating such, he only bowed to Austin and walked away.

"Lav, you have to understand that I do not have time for this."

"That is what you always say! But I won't let you push me aside again. I have been trying to have this conversation with you for days now and I won't leave this office until you tell me what you have planned."

A breath of frustration. "Lavender, please."

"No." A foot hit the floor, hard. "Tell me, Vincent. Or is it that you haven't planned anything at all?"

Austin pushed the door aside. The two occupants within didn't notice him. One of them he recognized as the man who had approached him last night, Mr. Vincent Latrice himself.

The other person was a lady, similar in appearance to Vincent. Her hair was a mousy brown that was pulled back into a chignon, a few tendrils framing her face. She clutched a book to her chest, her slight frame draped in a brown dress that did not complement her well. She didn't seem to care about that, however.

She looked so...normal. Not exactly what Austin was picturing and yet not surprising either. Had they been in a room full of people, she would have become a wallflower.

"Vincent, you promised!" Despite the plainness of her appearance, her voice was full of life, even though it was frustrated. "Father promised and you promised to uphold it when he died."

"Lavender, I know." Vincent pinched the bridge of his nose. "I'm working on it, all right."

"How? Just tell me anything and I will leave you alone." When her words were met with silence, she seized Vincent's sleeve. "The London Season has begun and yet I have nothing to—"

"If you don't mind," Austin cut in, leaning against the door frame. "I would like to get on with my meeting with Mr. Latrice."

The lady—Lavender—whirled to face him with a gasp. Looking at her full on stole Austin's breath for a moment. Her chocolate brown eyes were vivid with emotions, surprise and then confusion and then annoyance washing over her face in such clarity that Austin doubted she was capable of hiding her thoughts.

"Who are you?" With that book still clutched to her chest, she approached him, looking him up and down. Unlike the butler, she only looked curious rather than uptight. "How did you get in here?"

Austin tilted his head at her, surprised at himself for nearly responding. Then he met Vincent's eyes over her head. "Shall we?"

"My lord, I did not expect to hear from you so soon." The distress that had consumed Vincent before was gone, a smile on his face. "Come, come. Have a seat. Let me pour you a drink."

"But Vincent—"

"Lavender, we can continue this conversation another time. And I promise you, when that time comes, I shall answer all your questions, all right?" Vincent approached her, ushering her towards the door.

Lavender pouted, looking back and forth between Austin and Vincent. She looked just about ready to argue but then Vincent said, "Not in front of guests, Lav. Or have you forgotten your lessons?"

She thinned her lips at that, narrowing her eyes at Vincent. For a moment, Austin was certain that she would continue to argue. He was oddly looking forward to it.

But then she sighed heavily, sending a scathing look in Austin's direction. Up close, she was far smaller than him and yet she glared him down as if she were twice his size. "I hope you know that I find it quite rude of you to interrupt another's conversation in that manner."

Austin tilted his head to the side, his irritation mounting. This had already gone on for much longer than he cared for. "I do not care what you think."

"That comes as no surprise to me, considering your propensity for impudence, sir," she shot back without a second of hesitation, taking Austin by surprise. "But I'll have you know that the only reason I am leaving is because I have better things to do than waste time in your presence. I have important matters to deal with, like the ending of my book. But I'm sure you would know nothing about that."

Austin frowned at that. Did she just imply that he could not read?

Before he could think of a reply, Vincent stepped in between them with a sheepish grin. "Please do not mind her. She is quite used to getting what she wants. Lavender, please leave."

Her cheeks grew red, her shoulders rigid with mounting tension. Vincent grasped both her shoulders and forcefully guided her out the door. She didn't let up her glare however, burning holes into Austin until the door closed in her face.

Austin let out a breath, raking a hand through his hair. "Let us get this over with, Mr. Latrice. I have come here regarding your...contract. Or whatever you deem this to be." He pulled out the folded piece of paper and rested it on a mantle nearby. "In it, you state that you wish for me to marry your sister, but surely you cannot be serious."

Vincent faced him with a gleam in his eye. "It is exactly as it says, my lord. I wish for you to marry my sister, Lavender by the end of the Season."

Chapter Two

Austin had to sit down. He usually considered himself a strong man, mentally and physically. Capable of handling the toughest situations he found himself in. But Vincent Latrice's words had a way of bringing home the reality of what he was about to get himself into and he had the uncomfortable notion that the ground was swaying under his feet.

He sank into the armchair next to the hearth, folding his fingers in front of him. Lavender Latrice. Mr. Vincent Latrice, one of the wealthiest men in England, wanted to marry his sister off to a bastard son of the late Earl of Derby. How mirthful.

"Why?" was Austin's first word after a minute of silent contemplation.

Vincent made his way over to the sideboard and began pouring two glasses of brandy. "It is simple, my lord. Lavender is now ten-and-eight years old. It is time for her to be married."

"But why me? You approached me in the dead of night at an illegal fighting ring to all but beg me to consider the offer. Why?"

Vincent's face gave nothing away as he approached. Austin wondered if this was his usual demeanor when working. "Before I answer your question, Lord Derby, I take it you are considering saying yes?"

Austin hesitated, then nodded. "I am. For my own personal reasons. But I need to be certain that I am not walking into a trap."

"I would have no reason to trap you, my lord."

"That is what someone who wishes to trap me would like for me to believe."

Vincent chuckled. He chose the armchair next to Austin, sitting in a familiar manner that instantly made Austin uncomfortable. He took the glass of brandy Vincent offered to him and immediately set it aside.

Vincent raised a brow at that but chose not to comment. Instead, he said, "Firstly, I appreciate your consideration. Considering the fact that your first meeting with my sister did not go as I anticipated, I was almost certain that you would reject me outright."

"That option is still on the table," Austin stated.

"Of course, so allow me to be plain. The only thing I request is that you accept Lavender as your betrothed for the duration of the Season and are wed by the end of it. However, you would be expected to perform your duties as her betrothed."

Austin raised a brow. "Which would be?"

"Escorting her to any event she is invited to. Lavender is quite the socialite, you see. She will expect to attend them all and I think she would fancy having a handsome gentleman as her escort."

"I'm sure you would have done a fine job yourself. Why do you need me for that?"

"Sadly, I do not have the time to attend to every one of my sister's wishes, as much as she would want otherwise. This way, you two could get to know each other a bit more, as well. I must also inform you that Lavender will expect a lavish wedding at the end of the Season. She's always dreamed of it, after all. Our father promised her that she would get it once she was at the age to be married and I took on that promise when he passed away. Lavender, as you could see, will not let me forget it."

Austin shifted uncomfortably in the chair. "The contract didn't state any of that."

"I did not want to scare you away," Vincent stated, sipping his brandy calmly.

Wise thinking. "Then I want double her dowry," Austin announced on a whim.

Vincent did not bat an eye. "Deal."

Austin didn't dare show his surprise. There was something about Vincent Latrice that put him on edge. As if the man saw more than he let on. "I do not understand you," Austin confessed. "If rumours are true, you are one of the wealthiest men in England. Why do you and your sister care so much about high society?"

"Do not get me wrong, my lord," Vincent answered and Austin resisted the urge to tell him to stop calling him that, "I do not care about such things. While I do understand the weight placed on having a title, I find that wealth moves mountains far more than prestige does. Lavender, however, has always dreamed about attending the London Season with the upper echelons of society since she was a little girl. Perhaps it has something to do with the books she reads. I'm not certain, nor do I intend to question it now. But you know how the ton can be, my lord."

"Do I?" Austin asked dryly, which made the merchant laugh again.

"You are far closer to them than we will ever be. Wealthy we may be, my lord, but we are nobodies. We have no titles. We have nothing that will guarantee us an invite to any of these events. You, on the other hand, will be issued an invite or two to a number of parties, soirees, and balls and I would like for you to bring Lavender with you to each one. As such, if you accept the terms of this agreement, your betrothal would have to be established quickly."

"You have thought this out quite thoroughly," Austin observed.

"You see how persistent Lavender can be. I had no choice. Now," Vincent leaned forward a little, "do we have a deal?"

Austin studied him for a moment. Vincent's face was perfectly neutral but his words were what gave him away. This was not just to fulfill a promise made by his father. He was going to such lengths because he loved his sister dearly, enough to approach a man like Austin and give him whatever he wanted if it meant his sister would be happy.

A kinder man would accept the terms as they were. A smarter man would capitalize on the small show of affection.

"I want the doubled dowry in full," Austin stated.

"If you so wish," Vincent responded without hesitation.

"I also want you to pay for the renovations of my properties out of pocket over the course of the Season. By the end of it, your sister and I shall have proper homes to start our lives in."

Something moved in Vincent's expression. Austin didn't miss that he hesitated for half a beat before saying, "I accept those terms."

Relief flooded Austin instantly, enough for him to reach a hand out and say, "We have a deal then."

Finally, a smile stretched across Vincent's face. "I'm glad to hear it. I shall begin the preparations right away."

Austin stood. There was no reason to stay here any longer. He'd gotten what he wanted out of this and that was to preserve the legacy his father had left behind, the one his stepmother had loved so much. His neglect of the family manor had gone on for too long but now things would begin to change.

"Just one more thing, my lord," Vincent said as he began leading Austin back to the door. "Would you happen to know of any titled young ladies looking for a husband?"

Austin blinked at him. A beat of silence went by before Vincent laughed awkwardly.

"I will take that as a no. No worries. I shall continue the search myself." He opened the door. "Thank you for taking the time to come, Lord Derby. My butler will escort you out."

Indeed, the butler was already standing on the other side as if he had been waiting for the meeting to be over. Austin instantly felt annoyed at the sight of him. "We'll be in touch, Mr. Latrice."

"Vincent, please. We will be family soon."

Austin only grunted at that, turned, and left.

Chapter Three

"What exactly do you think you're doing?"

Lavender gasped, then clamped a hand over her mouth. She whirled and came eye to eye with Henry, the butler. He had his usual unimpressed look on his face, looking down at her through his spectacles.

"Henry, hush!" she whispered frantically, backing away from the door of her brother's study. "They might hear you."

"They might hear you," Henry pressed. "Why are you pressing your ear against the door, miss? Were you eavesdropping?"

"Oh, of course I was!" Lavender said in an exasperated whisper. "And I cannot hear anything if you distract me like this."

Lavender approached the door again, pressing her ear against the cool wood. She could hear mumbling on the other end but could not make out specific words.

"Must I remind you, Miss Lavender, that it is quite unbecoming of a proper lady to eavesdrop on others' conversation," came Henry's judgmental voice once more. "You may not hold a title but you are the mistress of this house and, as such, you are expected to conduct yourself like one."

Lavender sighed again, moving away from the door. "I hardly think it is—" She broke off at the stern look Henry gave her. It took everything in her not to roll her eyes. "Very well. But please let my brother know that as soon as he is done with his meeting with that brute of a man, he should come and see me in the drawing room."

"I shall pass on the message."

Lavender took up the book she'd left on a side table and held it to her chest once more, setting off down the hall. She glanced over her shoulder to see Henry still standing there, watching her leave. It seemed he had no intentions of letting her sneak back to listen. She supposed she would just have to bombard her brother with questions when she saw him next.

Lavender made her way to the drawing room and flopped over into her favorite chaise lounge under the open bay window. A gentle breeze wafted over her face as she opened her book to the last page she'd read. But after a few seconds, she realized it was fruitless trying to focus. All she could think about was that impudent man barging in on her conversation with Vincent.

"Who does he think he is?" she asked to no one in particular, sitting upright so quickly that her head spun.

Simply thinking about the short interaction was enough to make her blood boil. She'd never met such a rude man in her life! And Vincent had the gall to usher her out of the room as if that hadn't interrupted them! As soon as he was free she would give him piece of her mind.

She tried focusing on her book again and succeeded for a short while—until the door opened and her tired-looking brother walked in.

"Give me a second before you start asking me questions, Lavender," Vincent said just as she shot to her feet. "I need to prepare myself."

Lavender stayed quiet for three seconds—enough time for him to find a seat—before she could not hold back any longer. "Who was that man?" she demanded to know.

"That, my dear sister, was a the Earl of Derby."

Shock stilled her tongue. The Earl of Derby? The same Earl of Derby rumored to be the bastard turned heir of the late earl's estates? What in God's name was he doing meeting with her brother?

She didn't realize she'd asked the question out loud until Vincent said, "We were discussing you, actually."

"Me?" Lavender repeated.

"More specifically, your betrothal to the earl." Vincent grinned at her but Lavender could only stare at him.

Seconds of silence stretched on for so long that Vincent sat up straighter, frowning in concern. "Lavender? Are you all right?"

"I might have heard you incorrectly," Lavender said in a soft tone. "Did you say that the Earl of Derby is meant to be my betrothed?"

"He is your betrothed," Vincent pressed. "We finished working out the details but that is the result of it, yes. You will get your wish, Lav. By the end of the Season, you will have your big and beautiful wedding."

"To the earl..."

"Yes, to the earl. Is something the matter?"

Lavender's legs gave out beneath her. She sank onto the chaise lounge, her breath whooshing from her lungs. This couldn't be...How could her brother expect her to be married to a man like him?

"Do you even know him, Vincent?" Lavender asked, still reeling.

"I do not need to know him well," Vincent explained. "Many lords and ladies marry each other without even meeting beforehand. In this case, you will be betrothed and get to know each other during the course of the Season, before your wedding. Isn't that what you've always wanted?"

"I did not mean for you to shackle me to a gentleman whose first words to me were ruder than anything I have ever heard before!"

Vincent frowned at that. "You sound displeased, Lav."

Lavender shook her head, trying to reign in the overwhelming horror she felt at this news. Her brother was trying, at least. After all this time, when it felt as if he always had more important things to do than heed his promise to her, it was a step in the right direction. But if that meant she was heading straight to the earl then perhaps they needed to take a few steps back.

"I ask again, Vincent," she said as calmly as she could. "Do you know who he is?"

"If you are referring to his former status as a bastard then yes, I am aware."

"What will others say if I am to be the bride of a gentleman who was once a bastard?"

"They will say nothing because he is no longer one. He is the Earl of Derby and no amount of rumours will change that." Vincent pinched the bridge of his nose, looking weary. Lavender hated whenever he put that expression on his face. "Give it some time, Lav. You will come around to the idea, and to him, in time."

Lavender swallowed her protests. She seriously doubted it. Being the earl with such rumors attached to their name was one thing. But he had already proven himself to be nothing but a rude brute with no proper upbringing. Lavender couldn't promise that she would stay civil in his presence, let alone marry him!

But she was getting what she wanted finally after all this time. A step into the life of the upper class, though tethered to the earl. At least now she would be able to enjoy the London Season and the intricacies of elite company the way she'd always seen in the books.

Perhaps it would not be as bad as she thought. God she prayed that was the case.

Chapter Four

This might have been a mistake.

Austin couldn't recall how many times he'd thought that since he'd left Latrice Manor yesterday afternoon. Now that he was back the next day, the thought ran through his mind with increasing speed and urgency.

Everything had changed. It was a little alarming how quickly everything moved. Vincent Latrice had made good on his promise to pay double Lavender's dowry up front. Austin had barely had enough time to meet with his steward to assist with the allocation of the funds. But it was so much money that Austin felt a little unsteady now that he could go about with a full wallet.

Perhaps that would have been enough to put a smile on his face. But forcing himself to dress up this afternoon, hire a new coachman, and head to the Latrice Manor to meet with his new betrothed, was enough to put him in the foulest of moods.

Come and see me at noon. Lavender.

The note he'd received early this morning had been simple yet bossy. Austin already resented the fact that he had to heed her request. He was a man of his word, even if he was beginning to wonder if the money he'd received was worth doing all of this.

"Welcome, my lord." The uptight butler greeted him formally upon opening the door and it took all of Austin's strength not to shove right past him. "Miss Lavender is expecting you."

"Let us get this over with then," he grumbled under his breath. He brushed past him, shaking off the feeling of discomfort that settled in his bones.

"Please, follow me then." It seemed the butler didn't care to hide his distaste. Austin caught a glimpse of disdain in his eyes before he turned and made his way toward the sweeping staircase that sat to the left of the foyer.

Austin ignored him, his attention drawn to the ornate paintings lining the walls. A keener eye might have been able to determine the value of the pieces but it seemed rather expensive to Austin's untrained eye as well. His discomfort only grew as he studied the gold-lined banister of the staircase and intricate carvings in the wooden floor when they came to the landing. It seemed as if the Latrice family was content to display their wealth in every manner they could.

They may not be a part of the upper class, Austin thought, but he doubted they were any different. The butler brought him down a long hallway with far too many large mahogany double doors. Austin couldn't fathom why anyone would need this many rooms. Even Derby Estate in Bath was not this large, though the land surrounding the manor outshone that of Latrice Manor in droves.

At long last, the butler came to a stop in front of yet another massive double door and knocked. "Miss Lavender? Lord Derby is here to see you."

"Send him in!" came an urgent voice from the other end.

The butler turned and bowed to Austin. Austin scratched the back of his head, resisting the urge to turn and walk right back the way they came. He would never get used to such displays of reverence.

"Please call if you need me, my lord," the butler said, sounding rather humble considering the way he had looked at Austin just a few minutes prior.

Austin didn't bother to respond. He waited until the butler walked away then faced the door again. He didn't want to go in. He would much rather be anywhere else but here.

But duty called, he supposed.

Austin grasped both handles of the door and opened them at once. The chamber that met his eyes was the very playpen of affluence. Austin wouldn't be surprised if he learned that the Queen's chambers were no different.

A living area greeted him first, furnished generously with plush armchairs and chaise lounges with a beautiful fire crackling in the hearth. Two doors led away from the living space—one of which was slightly ajar. When Austin wandered further into the room, he caught sight of an armoire and the end of a bed. The other door was closed.

Miss Lavender was nowhere to be found. Annoyance prickled at his spine. He thought about calling out for her, then considered just leaving next.

Before he could make the decision, the closed door flew open. Miss Lavender came rushing out with her hair tumbling around her shoulders, a frown on her face.

"What is taking you so long?" she asked. "Come, come."

Without waiting for a response, she rushed back into the room, leaving the door ajar.

God help me.

The room was a small library with a writing desk sitting in the center. Miss Lavender was not seated at the desk however, nor at any of the armchairs perched in front of the bookshelves. She sat on the ground, hunched over a small book with papers scattered all around her.

She looked...different. Still as plain as when he met her, he noted. But between the unruliness of her mousy brown hair, her hunched posture, and her bare feet, she seemed less like a wealthy lady and more like a maid.

She looked up at him and that frown was back. "Will you continue to stand there, my lord?" she asked, her tone softening the bite of her words. "Come and sit."

"On the floor?" Austin asked without thinking.

She blinked as if she hadn't expected such a question. "Well, you can choose any of the seats if you so wish. But come close. I want to show you something."

Austin stayed by the door out of pure, natural stubbornness. "I am fine where I am," he said, crossing his arms. "Now why did you call me here? I must inform you that I have more pressing matters at hand than to cater to your every whim and command."

"Do you?" she asked with a raise of a brow. Austin only glared at her and she rolled her eyes. "I shan't be long. There is something I wanted to share with you."

Miss Lavender got to her feet and approached, taking her book with her. Austin was surprised at how lovely she smelt when she got close. Like fresh flowers after the rain.

"I have been up all night, you see," she began to explain. "That is why I look so haggard, but I could not sleep. I have been planning instead."

"I suppose you want me to ask you about what you were planning," he drawled, unable to hold back his irritation.

"Not to worry, my lord. I plan to say it anyway." She responded to him with such quickness that it threw Austin for a second. He wasn't used to that. "You see, my plan is a simple one but one I have been thinking about for years. Now that I am old enough to attend the London Season, I can finally do what I have always dreamed of doing. I will usurp Lady Amelia Howard and become the face of the upper class overnight!"

A grin stretched across her face, her brown eyes gleaming with excitement. Austin couldn't help the derisive look that crept over his face. "Should I know who that is?"

The grin fell. "You do not know Lady Amelia Howard? You are an earl! You should—" She broke off, pinching the bridge of her nose. "Never mind. Lady Amelia Howard is the Countess of Lively and the most popular person in all of England. Everyone—upper class or not—knows who she is. She holds the key to the gates of social acceptance, capable of turning a lady into a diamond or an outcast."

"And you want to impress her?" Austin asked slowly.

"I don't want to simply impress her. I want to *become* her."

Austin nearly laughed. He didn't think Miss Lavender was hearing herself. If this lady was as famed as she made her out to be, then the haggard-looking woman who'd seemed content to sit bare-footed and cross-legged in front of him mere seconds go was the last person capable of replacing someone of such a status.

The fire in Miss Lavender's eyes, however, intrigued him enough to keep him from pointing out how foolish she sounded. He looked down at the book she still had in her hand. Without warning, he plucked it from her fingers.

"My lord!"

Austin raised the book high above his head as he read. Miss Lavender tried to grab it but her small stature barely brought her halfway.

"'In the end, I shall have everyone in the ballroom applauding me'," he read in an incredulous tone. "How...creative."

She tugged on his arm with both her hands, then snatched the book from him. "It is quite rude stealing from others, my lord," she snapped. "And it would make no sense for you to read my plan in pieces. The reason I have called you here is because I wanted to go through everything with you. My brother informs me that we are to be wed and—"

"This matters not to me."

Her cheeks grew red in her frustration. "Please stop cutting me off. As I was saying, Vincent has informed me that we are now betrothed and that you have promised to escort me to every event I am invited to."

Austin gritted his teeth, wishing he could deny that truth. His silence had her nodding in satisfaction. She turned and began gathering the scattered pieces of paper into a stack before dumping it in his hands.

"Read up then," she urged. "And we shall determine how we go on from there."

Austin instantly sat the papers down on a nearby table. "I shall do no such thing."

"Very well then," she said as if she'd anticipated such a response. "We shall do one item. We shall take a stroll through Hyde Park while I inform you of what is to be expected. You, of course, will try your best to look increasingly captivated by me."

Austin stared at her for a few seconds. "I shall do no such—"

"Perfect! I shall get ready while you wait for me in the drawing room. Henry?"

All of a sudden, the butler was standing behind him. Austin bit back a curse.

"Yes, Miss Lavender?" he answered with a slight bow.

"Please escort Lord Derby to the drawing room and have a carriage prepared. We will be going for a promenade in short order."

"As you wish, miss."

Austin didn't get the chance to argue. Miss Lavender drifted by him, scooping up the papers as she went, and made her way to the other side of the room where her bedchamber was. He could only stare after her in disbelief.

"After you, my lord," the butler—Henry—spoke again.

It seemed he had no choice. Austin tried not to grumble about it as he left her chambers, reminding himself that this was what he had signed up for.

But had he known that he would be shackling himself to a spoilt aspiring socialite, he would have turned and run as fast as he could.

Chapter Five

Lavender didn't like it when things didn't go as planned. She was used to detailing every step she made, ensuring that she always put her feet in the right spot. So when there was a single misstep, especially if it was out of her hands, it felt as if everything was crashing down around her.

When that happened, all she could do was breathe. In and out. Take a step back. Reassess the situation and figure out what to do next.

But with the Earl of Derby standing in front of her, she hadn't a clue how to forward.

It seemed the scowl was permanently fixed on his face. Lavender tilted her head to the side as she watched him speak to the coachman. She hadn't a clue what they were conversing about and she didn't care. The mere fact that she'd convinced him to escort her to Hyde Park was a feat in and of itself. Though he might describe it as forcing rather than convincing...

Even so, it was a step in the right direction that they were here together, even if everything else had gone wrong. That long plan she'd written out months before she turned ten-and-eight—and had tweaked now and again—was currently under review all because of the man she was now betrothed to.

Lavender had expected her brother to follow through on his promise. She just hadn't quite expected it to be to a gentleman like the earl.

***

Lord Derby nodded to the coachman and then began making his way to her. His steps were long and commanding, his hands tight into fists at his sides as if he was always prepared to throw a punch. That scowl on his face did not hide his natural handsomeness. When he didn't speak, she could at least admire that he was pleasant to look at. Those deep green eyes, that sharp jawline, and his plush lips could make a lady's heart flutter if he didn't look as if he hated every human being within a mile of him. And he was dressed far finer than he had been yesterday, the cut of his waistcoat and breeches clinging to his large, muscular build.

Quite a handsome man, she thought as he drew closer. *It is a shame his personality is so sour.*

"What are you looking at?" he snapped the moment he made it up to her.

Lavender resisted the urge to sigh. Her brother had truly made the next few months far more difficult than she'd expected them to be. "I am looking at you, my lord. Was it not obvious?"

His scowl, as impossible as she thought it was, deepened. "Why?"

"I was observing you. You will make things quite difficult for me, you know."

"What are you talking about?"

She could not hold back her sigh this time. The park was rather populated at this hour and they were standing quite close to the road. It wouldn't do to stand around her any longer.

Lavender took a step towards him and slipped her arm through his. She felt him stiffen and begin to pull away but she whispered under her breath, "Do not pull away, or else you will cause a scene."

He didn't pull back but his arms laid stiffly against his side. "No one is looking at us to even notice."

"That is what you think," she pressed. "But they are always looking. And once you misstep, it will be spoken about for days to come. I didn't come here to cause a scandal, my lord. I came here to set my plan in motion and brief you on all the things you need to do."

"Dearest Lord, pray tell me what tangled web have I unwittingly ensnared myself in?" he muttered under his breath.

"Language," Lavender chastised. She schooled her expression into a more pleasant one, even though her annoyance was now sending heat to her cheeks. As discreetly as she could, she tugged on his arm and hoped that he would catch the hint.

Thankfully, he didn't protest this time. He bent his arm to accommodate hers and allowed her to lead him down a less traveled path, though they were still well within view of everyone else.

"To answer your question, my lord, I was observing you," Lavender went on. "Admiring you, to an extent. Though you did make it quite difficult with your crass manner of speech."

"It's how I've always spoken," he grunted. "No one has ever complained before."

"Perhaps they have just been too frightened," she mused. "In any case, I shan't allow you to frighten me nor will you deter me from my plan."

"To usurp that countess."

"Yes, that countess. *The* countess," she pressed. "But in order for my goal to come to fruition, I need your compliance."

"I am here walking with you," he grumbled. "What more do you want?"

"Well, for one, I would like for you to look a little happier to be here." Lavender peered up at him, giving him a soft smile. "Like this."

Lord Derby looked down at her as if she were an alien creature. "Don't do that."

Lavender's smile fell. It took everything in her not to give in to her irritation. Surely, this man was difficult.

"We'll get there," she said, mostly to herself. "I suppose I shouldn't be too surprised at your personality. I will just have to learn how to use it to my advantage."

"You know nothing about my personality," he protested.

"I know more than you think. Last night, after Vincent informed me of our arranged betrothal, I had my maid tell me everything she knew about you."

She could sense his surprise, even though her attention remained on the beaten path before her. "Your maid?" he growled in question.

"Yes, my lady's maid. Her name is Betty and she is quite talkative once she is comfortable. Since there is a divide between new money and old, I am unable to garner as much information about you as I would have if I had been born with a title, sadly. But servants tend to talk amongst themselves, you know, no matter who they work for. And she had a lot to say about you."

"I hear a lot of judgment coming from the lady whose only ambition is to become a part of a class of people who only want to exclude her."

How typical. He thought she was nothing but a simple-minded lady with no interest but to attend parties and climb up the social ladder. She supposed she couldn't fault him for assuming such, but it still bothered her.

Lavender rolled her eyes at his sarcastic drawl. "It isn't that simple."

"Oh, pray tell, my fair lady, how complex it is."

"My ambitions do not rest in being accepted by the ton alone, my lord," Lavender expressed, struggling to keep her tone civil. "I want to infiltrate the very same ton that humiliated my father at his most vulnerable moment and caused him to live in shame for the rest of his life. I will make them remember that moment and then regret it until the day they die. They will know the error of their ways and they will know it by my hand. And if I am given a gentleman like you to help me then I suppose I have no choice but to take it."

"A gentleman like me? Why on earth do you think I will assist you with any of this nonsense?"

"Because you have reason to invest in my ambitions," she stated. "You are a bastard, after all."

***

You are a bastard, after all.

The words rang through Austin's head like a gong. Every bone in his body went rigid, his heart instantly banging against his chest at a rapid pace. Emotions he could hardly contain raced through his body—horror, surprise, rage.

He settled on the rage. That was easy. That was something he was used to.

Austin pulled away from her and then caught Miss Lavender's elbow. She gasped in alarm—or perhaps pain—but it didn't stop him from dragging her off the path behind a large willow tree.

"Are you mad?" she gasped, eyes wide and cheeks red. She looked frantically around them. "Do you know how scandalous it would be if we were caught behind here by ourselves? We must be within view at all times!"

He couldn't believe his ears. This maddening woman had the gall to say such a thing after calling him a bastard right to his face?

"I do not give a damn what anyone thinks," he growled. "And clearly you do not either."

Miss Lavender pulled her arm from his grasp and took a step back, frowning in confusion. She pulled her shoulders back as if she was preparing herself for a fight. "You will have to be a little clearer than that if you want me to understand what you're referring to," she said stiffly.

"A bastard," he pushed through gritted teeth. "How bold of you to say that to my face."

"Is it not what you are?" she said. She seemed to catch herself, then draw in a deep breath. "Forgive me. It was what you were."

A harsh laugh barked from his throat, making her stiffen. He stalked away from her, running his hand through his hair. He couldn't understand the frustration that consumed him. Austin always knew his birthright. Everyone in England knew that the late Earl of Derby had been unfaithful to his wife with a maid and he had been the result of it. Once upon a time, he'd carried the title of a bastard like weight on his shoulders. More recently, he liked to think that he wore it like a badge of honor.

But hearing her referring to him as one with such gumption, something that he hadn't heard since he'd been in school, threw him. His title as an earl did not matter to his lady. Only his former status as a bastard did.

"I did not mean it as a slight, my lord," Miss Lavender spoke again. She had the audacity to speak as if he was the one misunderstanding her. "I only thought to be transparent with you. We could work together to—"

"You forget yourself, miss," Austin snapped, barely keeping his voice under control. She stiffened but didn't step back when he advanced on her, tilting her head to meet his eyes. "I am not here to cater to your petty need for revenge. So while I may not be the gentleman you are hoping for, I am not a tool to be used for your purposes either. My only interest was to marry you and then continue with my life as if you do not exist."

She thinned her lips. Somehow, anger brought her face to life. A fire to her deep brown eyes, redness to her cheeks, the pink of her tongue darting out before she bit her bottom lip as if she were struggling to hold back the words she truly wanted to say.

"I apologise—" she began but Austin didn't care to stick around to hear the rest of it.

"I have had enough of this," he muttered to himself, then turned and headed back the way they came.

He didn't think she would come after him. He walked briskly and Miss Lavender would have to run to catch up to him. So when he made it halfway to the carriage, though he had no intention of taking it, he was surprised when she caught his arm. There was enough force within her grasp to stop him.

"You will receive an invitation later tomorrow for tea hosted by Mrs. Heather Lawrence at their family manor. You will be expected to escort me."

Austin curled his upper lip in disgust, pulling his arm away from her. He ignored the pinch of disappointment at her words. He'd expected another attempt at an apology but her mind was focused on one thing alone, it seemed. Like every other vapid lady in London.

He didn't respond, stalking away instead. He had half a mind to go straight to Vincent Latrice and tell him that he could no longer do this. Had it not been for the weight of money in his wallet, he would have.

Chapter Six

She was going to kill him. And Vincent. And perhaps even the lords and ladies of the ton who made her feel the need to put herself through this in the first place.

Anxiety coursed through Lavender's body like a roaring river. She smoothed her hands over her dress for the tenth time even though she knew that there wasn't a single thing out of place. She'd chosen her dress perfectly, a subtle green color that hopefully brought out the depth of her eyes with a matching pair of gloves. Betty had curled her hair in lovely ringlets with a simple floral headpiece affixed between them. Her aim was to look effortlessly put together like many other ladies she'd witnessed before but she could hardly pull that off when she had been waiting for her chaperone to show up for the past thirty minutes.

She glanced out the window of her carriage once more, resisting the urge to shake her leg in impatience. Of course the earl was late. If she hadn't received a curt letter last night informing her that he would be attending, she would have assumed that he wasn't coming at all.

Lavender didn't dare to exit her carriage until he arrived. She asked her coachman to wait near Lawrence Manor so that no one would know that she had arrived yet. It would be better if they both arrived late rather than one at a time. But she didn't know how much longer she could hold out.

Just when she thought she couldn't take it any longer, she spotted a familiar figure ambling down the street. Lavender quickly exited the carriage, grabbing her skirts just in time to keep everything in place. She watched as Lord Derby made his way to the manor with his hands tight into fists at his side and that scowl on his face. He walked with a slight limp as if he was injured.

And oh dear, what happened to his face?

Lavender's jaw went slack when he came to stop in front of her. She couldn't find the right words. There were just too many things going wrong right now. His lateness. The dusty, out-of-fashion clothes he wore. And worse of all, the purple-black bruise encircling his right eye.

"What happened to you?" she breathed in alarm.

Lord Derby didn't deem that a question he should answer. He only grunted in annoyance and walked by her. To her horror, he was walking right up to the front door of the manor. Lavender grabbed her dress and hurried behind him.

"You cannot go in like that," she said hurriedly. "Who did that to you? Why do you have a blackened eye? My lord, you cannot."

He said nothing. He only raised the knocker and banged it hard on the front door, twice. Lavender thought she might melt in embarrassment.

Nothing was going according to plan. *Breathe in, breathe out.*

Before she could say anything else, the door opened to a slightly confused-looking butler. Lavender plastered a smile on her face, her heart fluttering when the butler looked from Lord Derby to her and then back to him.

"Good afternoon, Mr. Jenkins," she greeted. "I hope your day is going well?"

"Quite so, Miss Lavender." The confused Mr. Jenkins stepped to the side. "Please, if you would follow me."

She did just that, thankful that the earl was following along as well even though he was sporting a terrible bruise. She'd been to this manor often enough for the staff to know her well, and the other way around. Mr. Jenkins was not the sort of man who showed his emotions very often, so he must truly have been shocked to have looked at them like this.

And if he was then she could only imagine how everyone was going to react when they entered. The fact that they were late only made it worse. It meant everyone would be present to witness their entrance. Had everything gone as planned, she would have welcomed that.

Her nervousness shot through the roof as they drew closer to the dining room. Lavender could hear the hum of chatter on the other end which meant the tea party was well underway. She drew in a deep breath then put that pleasant expression she'd practiced on her face. She glanced up at Lord Derby and was not surprised to see that he looked as if he would much rather be anywhere but here.

The moment they entered, the party seemed to stop. The soothing notes from the pianoforte being played in the corner continued, of course, but all eyes fell on them and all conversation ceased. Lavender made sure her soft smile didn't slip even when she saw her friend, Alice, take a step in her direction in the corner of her eye. Instead, she took Lord Derby by the arm and steered him towards a relatively uncrowded section of the refreshments table.

"You have only one task this afternoon," she whispered between her tight smile. "And that is to act as if I am the apple of your eye and you cannot wait to be married to me."

"You ask a lot of me," he grumbled.

"It shouldn't be too hard." Lavender skimmed her gaze over new and old faces, men and women she would have to convince of her ruse. "You need only smile at everything I say and say nice things about me. Lie straight through your teeth if you have to."

He made a derisive sound. Lavender didn't have to look at him to guess that he was rolling his eyes. "Surely you see that it is madness to go to such lengths to impress strangers."

"They are not strangers." Lavender picked up a cucumber sandwich and handed it to him, that smile still fixed on her face. "Not all of them. My dear friend Alice is the one who is hosting this party and I do not want her to know what we are doing. Not yet. I love her to death but she is rather blunt and tends to speak without thinking."

"Sounds oddly familiar."

"Oh, hush," she hissed. "And smile. Someone is approaching."

He did no such thing, which sent her irritation through the roof. It took Lavender every bit of her strength to straighten her spine and smile at the person who approached, relief flooding her when she saw who it was.

Colin Asher looked more handsome than the last time she'd seen him. Their fathers had been friends and so Lavender had all but grown up with him. As they grew into adulthood, they'd spent less time with each other, but Lavender was still as good at reading his expressions as she had been when they were younger.

And right now, she saw nothing but confusion. Hopefully he wasn't as good as seeing through her as she was him.

"Lavender," he greeted, eyes softening for a moment. "I have been waiting for you to arrive. Don't tell Alice but I have been dreadfully bored without you."

A genuine laugh bubbled up her throat and she relaxed a little. "I am not surprised, Colin. But you must learn not to keep me around for your entertainment, you know. We are far too old for such things."

"Yes, so I am beginning to see." His kind blue eyes fell on Lord Derby and a tiny frown pulled at his brows. "I'm sorry, I do not think we have met."

Lavender waited for the earl to respond. A second went by. Then another. Before it could get too uncomfortable, she spoke up. "This is Lord Austin Thomas, the Earl of Derby. He is my betrothed."

"Betrothed?" Colin echoed, eyes growing wide.

"Yes, I know it is quite surprise. I can hardly believe it myself." That much was true. Lavender still laid awake at nights wondering if this truly was what her life had become.

"Hm." Colin's frown only grew deeper as he faced Lord Derby. Lavender felt a twinge of trepidation. Colin was important to her, one of her dearest friends. She didn't want to have to deal with contention between the two of them when she had more important things to focus on.

"Lord Derby, you say?" he went on, raising his chin. Was it her or did it look as if he was trying to make himself taller? If that were the case, it didn't work. Lord Derby's presence was enough to make the tallest man in the room appear like a dwarf. "I have heard you. You inherited your father's title."

"Smart of you to put that together," Lord Derby droned.

Lavender's heart leapt into her throat. This wasn't going to go well.

Colin's left eye twitched. "Were you the one who asked for Lavender's hand in marriage?"

"Why does it matter?"

"You must understand how sudden this is to me. I'm sure it matters not for you to tell me how it happened."

Lavender expected questions. She'd gone through every possible one beforehand and had a response that would not raise anyone suspicions. She didn't mind if others believed that it was an arranged marriage because that was the norm of the upper class. It could even help to get her integrated much faster.

What she did not expect was the hostility brewing between Lord Derby and Colin. The earl stared him down and Colin matched that stare with increasing agitation, which surprised Lavender even futher. Colin had always been slow to anger. Already he looked just about ready to tackle Lord Derby to the ground.

"Vincent introduced us," Lavender cut in. "He thought we would make a nice match and well, I cannot say that I disagree."

"A nice match?" Colin repeated, not taking his eyes off the earl. "I am yet to see it. Especially since he is yet to respond to my question."

Lord Derby cocked his head to the side. Lavender didn't like the look in his eyes. Dark amusement? Annoyance? Anger? Whatever it was, it gave her a bad feeling.

"Why do you care?" Lord Derby asked.

"Because Lavender is my friend. I care about her, which makes me wonder if you are good enough for her."

"It does not matter if I am."

"Wha—of course it does!" Colin was shouting now. Others were beginning to look.

Lavender put a hand on his shoulder and fixed a smile on her face. She squeezed his shoulder, forcing him to look at her. "I appreciate your concern, Colin, but there is no need to worry."

Colin did not look very convinced. "I just think that—"

"My, my, what's going on here?" Miss Alice Lawrence swept into the conversation like a breath of fresh air. "Lavender, who is this handsome gentleman?"

Lavender could have kissed her for the distraction. Avoiding her now seemed like a foolish idea. Alice had always been good at keeping emotions mellow. "This is my betrothed, Alice," Lavender responded. "The Earl of Derby."

"Good day, Lord Derby," Alice greeted with a proper curtsy. "It is a pleasure to meet you."

Unlike Lavender, she had a natural ladylike demeanour that made her the queen of their peers. Lavender always emulated her whenever they were out. What came natural to Alice was always an act for Lavender and she admired her friend for it.

Lord Derby only grunted something unintelligible. Lavender tried not to scowl at him. Instead, she stepped in between the two men, forcing more distance between them, and embraced her friend. "This is a wonderful party, Alice. You outdid yourself, as always."

"I would have done a far better job if I had known you were bringing a guest with you," Alice said, tucking a stray blond curl behind her ear. She was a gentle beauty, with large brown eyes, honey-blond hair, and a heart-shaped face. Lavender had once envied her beauty when she had been young and insecure. It had been hard being the plain friend standing next to a diamond.

"I wanted to surprise you," Lavender told her.

"And surprise me you did." Alice clapped her hands excitedly. "Let us sit and enjoy some tea, shall we? I would love to get to know you a little better, Lord Derby."

Thankfully, Alice walked off without giving Lord Derby a chance to respond. Lavender would hate to have to think of something else to say when he inevitably didn't. Colin lingered for a moment before he trailed after Alice as well, leaving Lavender and Lord Derby behind.

"Can you at least pretend like you want to be here?" Lavender whispered to him.

"You're lucky I am even here."

That response was enough to frighten Lavender.

Alice chose a small table that was able to seat the four of them along with two men Lavender didn't know. She made sure that they sat as far away from Colin as possible, not wanting to risk another awkward confrontation.

Introductions were passed around quickly, tea was shared, and it didn't take long for Lavender to realize that everyone was curious about the earl by her side. She'd expected as much, had prepared for it. She had not, however, prepared for the question surrounding his bruises.

He was standoffish. He was cold. And as the conversation wore on, he was truly getting on top of her nerves.

Lavender caught three confused glances from Alice who had to be bursting at the seams with the urge to ask why they were getting married. And Lavender didn't know what to say to her when the time came. Right now, she was beginning to wonder if it would be better to just end this engagement altogether and walk this path by herself.

Just when she thought it couldn't get any worse, one of the men at the table—Mr. Henderson, Lavender believed—said, "Forgive me, my lord, but this has been bothering me for some time now. Do I know you from somewhere?"

Lord Derby barely glanced at him. His attention was focused on his third glass of wine, looking balefully at him as if he was wishing he had something stronger. "Is that so."

Sensing another horrible and uncomfortable conversation, Lavender jumped in. "Perhaps you mistake him for someone else, sir," she said with a lighthearted laugh. "Lord Derby is quite the recluse, you see. He does not partake in society very often."

"How did you meet then?" Colin asked. "If he is such a recluse."

Lavender tried not to scowl at him. If she didn't know any better, she would think he was purposely trying to uncover their ruse.

"A party, perhaps?" Alice offered. She must have sensed Lavender's hesitation.

To her surprise, Lord Derby scoffed. "I shall not be seen at such occasions under any circumstances. I have no interest in spending time with the ton."

"Is that so?" Mr. Henderson leaned closer, eyes glittering with intrigue. "But I know I must have seen you somewhere. I wonder where it is. It will bother me all evening if I do not figure it out."

"I'm sure he—"

"If you're so sure then there's only one possible place I can think of," Lord Derby said, cutting Lavender off.

"Oh?" Mr. Henderson perked up. "And where would that be?"

"The docks."

The other man blinked. Everyone else looked just as confused—and Colin was simply suspicious. Lavender debated cutting in and ending this before it got any further, not trusting where the earl was going with this.

"The docks?" Colin questioned. "What purpose would you have at the docks?"

"Are you involved with the shipping industry, perhaps?" Alice asked, sipping her tea daintily.

Lord Derby drained his glass and wrung his neck. "The docks is where I participate in prizefighting."

Chapter Seven

Lavender didn't know what to do at that moment. The silence that descended upon the table was thick enough to slice through bread, so uncomfortably judgmental that she felt cold sweat wash her entire body.

Fighting. The man she was set to marry, whose arm she had entered the room on, had just told a room full of people that his favorite past time was fighting. If she hadn't already been seated, Lavender would have fainted right there.

Instead, she licked her lips and tried to think of what to do. No one spoke as if they were waiting for her to say what she felt about it. And the earl continued eating as if nothing were amiss, as if he hadn't just thrown yet another wrench in her plans.

She stood suddenly, hands curling at her sides. She didn't have to fake her anger. It rumbled throughout her body with such force that she had to resist from doing what she truly wanted to do. Aware that many eyes were on her, Lavender didn't dare turn to her betrothed and tell him exactly what she thought about his announcement. Instead, she marched off and prayed he had the good sense to follow behind her.

Within four seconds, she realized that her hopes were foolish. She didn't hear footsteps behind her, didn't hear the scrape of the chair to indicate that anyone had stood. Silence trailed behind her as she marched to the door and struggled to fight back tears of anger.

It took every strength in her body to keep from slamming the door in her frustration. Vincent would certainly hear about this. Didn't he look into this man before he agreed to their betrothal? Surely this should have been a topic of conversation at some point in their discussion?

Lavender stalked away, rage trembling with such force through her limbs that she had to distance herself from the dining room door, not trusting herself not to do anything foolish. She had to think of a way to fix this. Her reputation amongst her peers was in jeopardy and, if she wanted to reach the very top, this wasn't the start she needed. Indeed, after all her preparations, her dreams could not go down the truth like this.

She heard a door open. Lavender stilled, listening to the ensuing silence with her heart in her throat. Did Alice come after her? She loved her friend dearly but she wasn't in the mood to face the humiliation she'd just suffered.

Footsteps started towards her. Lavender blinked back her tears of anger and tried to school her expression into something more civil. Putting on her usual mask to hide the lady underneath.

"Lavender," came a breathless voice behind her.

Lavender turned in surprise. It wasn't Alice nor the earl. To her surprise, it was Colin Asher.

He was breathing a little heavily as if he had raced after her in the spur of the moment. His blond hair looked a little more tousled than usual, his thick brows knitted together in concern. He approached her in two quick steps, not hesitating to grasp her by the shoulders.

"Are you all right?" he asked her, scanning her face. The concern on his face was enough to warm the icy knot that had formed in the center of her chest.

"I suppose the easier thing to say would be that I am quite fine," she sighed.

Instead of laughing, like she'd expected him to do, Colin only frowned harder at her, his lips set in an unamused line. It was unusual to see. Colin was always on the verge of laughter, finding humor in every situation. There was no better person to see her in this state than him, she thought. Like her, Colin was the only child of a wealthy merchant. Unlike her, his father was still alive and kicking.

They'd been friends for so long that Lavender thought she'd seen him in every state. But the look on his face right now wasn't anything she'd witnessed before.

"Colin, is everything—"

He caught her wrist and began pulling her down the hallway before she could finish her question. His grip was firm enough to keep her protest at bay. Lavender didn't even think twice about the fact that he was dragging her further away from the dining room and that they had no chaperone.

Colin pulled her into an unoccupied parlor and closed the door, his jaw tense. "Lavender, what are you doing with that man?"

Lavender frowned at him. "I beg your pardon?"

"The Earl of Derby," he clarified. "Surely you aren't truly betrothed to him?"

Lavender sighed, sinking into the nearest armchair with obvious exasperation. "Yes, that is so." *Unfortunately*, she thought glumly.

Colin ran his fingers through his hair in distress. "Why?' Haven't you heard of his reputation?"

"Clearly I have not, considering my surprise at his announcement." Lavender paused, raising her brow. "Is there anything else I should know?"

"It is a rather delayed time to ask such a thing, don't you think?"

His incredulous tone only increased her ire. Lavender shot to her feet, making her way to the door. "If you only wished to chastise me about a decision I cannot undo, Colin, then save it for another time. I am no mood for it right now."

He caught her wrist before she reached for the handle. It was firm enough to give her pause, to make her scowl at him. "I am only worried for you, Lavender," he said after a deep breath. "When I saw you entering the room by his side I couldn't believe that you would—"

"That I would what?"

Colin hesitated. Lavender pulled her wrist free and opened the door. She didn't have time for this. They shouldn't even be alone anyway. It had been fine when they were younger and had very little expectations placed on them. But they were both at an age where they should be married. She should be chaperoned at all times, not falling into old habits.

She didn't make it two steps out of the room before Colin came after her. "I'm worried about you, Lavender," he pressed.

Lavender stopped, turning to face him. The pitiful look on his face made her annoyance soften. "I understand, Colin. But there truly is not anything you need to worry about."

"How can I not? Lord Derby's name runs rampant amongst the ton, Lavender. They talk about his dangerous upbringing and how it shows itself in his pastimes. Not to mention the fact that his estate is in desperate need of repairs. Clearly, he only wishes to marry you for your dowry."

That stung, even though Lavender had already assumed the same. "Many marriages are borne from such a desire, Colin. This time would be nothing new."

"I refuse to accept that." He took a step towards her. "Do you really want to be tied to a man who only wants you for your fortune?"

I could not care less about such a thing, she wanted to say. Instead, she shrugged. "It is not ideal but nothing can be done about it now."

"That isn't true." Colin reached for her hand. This time, he held it gently, brushing a thumb across the back of it.

Lavender resisted the urge to pull away but she couldn't stop the frown that crept across her brow. "Colin…"

"You are a beautiful lady, Lavender," he went on. "You needn't settle on the likes of the Earl of Derby. Not when you have far more respectable options standing before you."

Lavender tried swallowing past the lump that suddenly clogged her throat. The air had shifted. The frustration and confusion she'd seen on his face and had heard in his voice was gone. Now there was something tender lingering behind his blue eyes that made her want to tuck her tail and run.

She couldn't think of a single thing to say in response. The quiet stretched on uncomfortably with her hand still limp in his even though she knew she should pull away. He seemed no more eager to break the silence, waiting for her response.

Just when she thought she couldn't take it anymore, she heard a familiar voice. "Lavender?"

That was Alice. Relief flooded Lavender like a tidal wave as she pulled away and turned to face her friend, who was just coming around the corner. She drew in a breath to greet her but her words died in her throat when she saw the Earl of Derby following behind her with that constant scowl on his face.

Chapter Eight

A megrim was brewing in the back of his head, the kind that would leave him helpless and prone all day. Austin fought it as best as he could but his rising annoyance at this situation he found himself in only exacerbated his condition.

One week ago, he had been content with his life. He hadn't known how much the estate meant to his late father and stepmother. He hadn't cared about his declining wealth. And he hadn't given a single thought to being married.

Now, he stood brooding in the corner of a quaint drawing room with his arms crossed watching as his *beloved* betrothed and her friend discussed him.

He hadn't expected prizefighting would have caused such contention. But then again, he'd spent nearly all his life not caring about what the upper class thought, even though his father insisted that he was one of them. Going to their schools and enjoying the luxury of being an earl's son—albeit a bastard one—had only done so much to change who he truly was. Surely this small, plain-looking woman didn't think that she could!

"Perhaps it is not as bad as we think?" Miss Alice was saying. Austin didn't mind her half as much as he did Miss Lavender. She seemed polite yet firm, and pretty enough to be endearing. Or perhaps he could only tolerate her because he was not betrothed to him. Surely it had taken quite some convincing for him to follow her here in the first place.

"Alice, it may very well be worse than what we think," Miss Lavender complained. She seemed not to care about any of the ladylike graces she'd displayed at the party anymore. She was slumped on a couch with her face buried in her hands. Austin rolled his eyes at the dramatic display.

"Well, it certainly wasn't made any better with Colin running after you like that," Miss Alice murmured as she paced back and forth. "What was he thinking?"

"He was just worried for me, that's all," Miss Lavender said without hesitation.

Austin's scowl deepened. Miss Alice had chased this Colin away as soon as she arrived, much to Austin's pleasure. He didn't like the man and he didn't know why. All he knew was that he'd noticed the way his eyes followed Miss Lavender wherever she went, as if Austin did not exist, and it had bothered him. Akin to a lost puppy, Austin thought, but even hounds have more shame.

He'd felt a sliver of annoyance when he'd followed after Miss Lavender and a great amount of satisfaction when he was sent back the way he came.

"Worry or not, it would only make things worse," Miss Alice insisted. "Surely he doesn't want you starting the London Season with a scandal following behind your name."

"It matters not, Alice. After Lord Derby's announcement, I don't think I have any reputation left."

Austin scoffed loudly. Both women turned to look at him. One with a frown and the other with a scathing glare that would have made him drop dead if he were made of weaker stuff.

"Pardon me, my lord," Miss Lavender hissed. "But it seems you are not aware of the trouble you have caused me."

"Trouble?" Austin shot back with a raised brow. "I fail to see how what I do in my free time affects you."

"Whatever you do affects me, my lord. My last name will be dropped for yours, my life in your hands. I will become your wife. Anything you do will most certainly fall back on me."

"You're only saying that because you think I have upset your plans to overthrow that countess."

Miss Lavender got to her feet, her hands curling into fists. It was alarming how quickly her presence took up the span of the room, her anger a force to be reckoned with. Austin met it unflinchingly.

"Yes, and even that!" she exclaimed. "After all I have told you, why would you think it a good idea to say such a thing so publicly?"

"Because it is not as serious as you proclaim it to be."

"Not as serious—" She broke off, looking at her friend as if she couldn't believe what she was hearing. Miss Alice only melted back to the wall. Miss Lavender faced him again. "You are an earl and you do not realise the implications of your confession?"

"It is not that I do not realise it," Austin answered calmly despite his irritation at her tone. "It is that I do not care."

"How can you not when it affects your life?"

"I do not let what others think about me affect me to such an extent. Perhaps you should try that as well."

Her face grew so red that Austin would not be surprised if she fainted. But she approached him instead, not stopping until she was just an arm's length away. "You will return to the dining room and tell everyone that you spoke in jest."

Austin glared at her but was saved from having to respond when Miss Alice chose that as her chance to speak. "That will never work," she said. "It will only look like you are trying to fix your mess. It is far too obvious."

"Nor does it matter if it will because I have no intention of doing such a thing," Austin added. "And I certainly do not care to stand here and listen to you berate the things I chose to do and say because they do not fit into your perfect little plan."

He stalked away from her. Equal parts annoyance and surprise coursed through his body when she trailed right after him. "You cannot leave," she insisted from behind. "Not until we have spoken."

"What is there left to talk about?" he couldn't help but ask, whirling to face her again.

She was far closer than he thought she would be. Or perhaps he had simply stopped too abruptly because she collided into his chest with enough force that he had to hold her shoulders to steady her. Her scent washed over, emptying his mind for a moment.

But then she stepped out of his hold, wiping an odd look off her face and replacing it with a determined one. Austin tensed.

"Very well. You do not have to do anything else this afternoon. As a matter of fact, I think it would be best if you remained quiet for the remainder of the party. It may very well be what is best. However," the daring woman stepped closer to him, like a gazelle creeping nearer to a lion, "I hope you know that I intend to have you on my arm for every other event I am invited to for the rest of the Season. Subject to change, of course."

Austin's first inclination was to protest. He didn't want to go, didn't want to endure this any longer than he needed to. But he'd signed a contract and he was a man of his word.

Miss Lavender must have seen the resignation on his face because a saccharine smile stretched across her lips. "Don't worry," she said. "I have a schedule."

That was all Austin needed to hear to be certain that this would be the longest months of his life.

Chapter Nine

"Is this to your liking, my lord?"

Austin barely glanced at the sheets of paper before him before his mind drifted back to the pair of determined brown eyes that had been haunting him all night. "Good," he grunted, reaching absentmindedly for his glass of whiskey and waving his butler away.

"But, my lord, you did not choose."

Austin grumbled something unintelligible as the warm liquor washed through his body. He couldn't focus on a single thing. Not the ruckus echoing through the townhouse as workmen traipsed in and our conducting repairs. Not his butler, who had been trailing after him all morning asking him asinine questions like what drapes he would like in the drawing rooms. He could not even concentrate on the fact that he had the day to himself, free from the pressures of an impending wedding and his needy betrothed.

All he could think about was Miss Lavender and her *schedule.*

Truly, he didn't think such a mundane word could cause such a visceral reaction in him. He shuddered as he lurched to his feet, wandering anxiously to the sideboard to pour himself another drink.

To his frustration, his butler shadowed him. "My lord, then is this to your liking?" he asked, showing Austin a swath of fabric.

Austin hardly looked at it, annoyed. "I do not care about such things," he grumbled. "Leave me be, won't you?"

The butler's hand fell to his side. "My lord, you had tasked me with the job of renovation. I hesitate to make a decision you may not like."

"Just keep everything the same then," he snapped, stalking to the window instead. "No changes. Tell them to make their repairs and change nothing in the process."

"Understood, my lord." Still, the butler hesitated. Austin could feel his eyes boring in the back of him without turning around.

"What is it?" Austin pushed through gritted teeth, already frustrated with whatever was to come.

"If I may make a suggestion, my lord—"

"You may not."

"Of course," the butler said quickly. But he remained, silent for just a few moments before he said, "I only wished to point out that you will be a married man soon. It is likely that the future Lady Derby will spend most of her time in the London house. Perhaps it would be a good idea to make changes that may better suit her taste."

Austin said nothing. He only turned slightly, fixing his glare on the butler. The other man stiffened and sank into a deep bow.

"Pardon me, my lord," he said hastily and all but scurried out of the room.

Alone, Austin did not feel any better. Between staff offering unsolicited advice and a mousy lady hounding his every thought, he was in a constant state of irritation. He could hardly be thankful for how quickly the repairs were being made. Soon enough, he could visit his family estate to see if it had returned to its former glory. That was the main reason he'd agreed to all of this madness in the first place, after all.

A schedule. That would not stop hounding him.

Austin reached into the breast pocket of his waistcoat and pulled free the sheet of paper folded within. Last night, Miss Lavender had eagerly pressed this into his palm, taking full advantage of his stunned state. She hadn't even seemed annoyed with him any longer. He couldn't help but wonder if she had meant to distract him with his irritation before making her announcement.

"Take a good look, my lord," she'd chirped. "And be ready when the days come."

Then she'd left him standing there, her friend giving him an apologetic smile as she left as if she too knew exactly what Miss Lavender had done.

A trap within a trap. And he'd walked right into both.

Austin sighed as he unfolded the letter and skimmed his gaze over the long, detailed list of events. Some were marked with an asterisk which she had explained meant she was yet to secure an invite. Everything listed, however, came with another set of instructions. What to wear, how to act, who to speak to.

He thought of Miss Lavender sitting on the floor of her library, pouring over this list with such detail. Her hair slung over one shoulder, ink smudged on her hands. A focus in her eyes that blocked out the world around her.

Why did a girl, with such obvious romantic ideals, agree to an arranged marriage?

He simply couldn't understand it. She was detailed, she was driven, and she romanticized the ton and the London Season. Wouldn't she have preferred to attend these events on her own and fall in love with a man on her own?

"Perhaps she knows how foolish such ideals are," he mumbled to himself, trudging over to his desk. He sank into his chair with a huff, tossing the list on the desk's surface. He rested his neck on the back of the chair, his eyes wandering to the portrait across the room over the mantle.

The late Countess of Derby had been a beauty in her youth. With natural blond ringlets and a pair of ice-blue eyes that made her the envy of her time, she'd once held the heart of nearly every man in London. Or, at least that was what the late earl had said. When she'd married the earl, it had broken the hearts of many.

Austin had learned early on in life that marriage was simply a show for others. Even if such a thing like love existed, it was not enough for a marriage to work. His stepmother's love for his father had only fizzled into underlying resentment when Ausitn came into this world. Even though she had accepted Austin like he was her own, she'd never forgiven her husband.

And his marriage would be no different. He didn't intend to be unfaithful like this father had been. No, he didn't want to be anything like his father. But that didn't mean he would be happy. That didn't mean he intended to nurture the relationship in any way. After the wedding, they would go their separate ways. A marriage in name only, like many others in London. He didn't even care about having an heir.

But until then, he had to adhere to his betrothed's foolish schedule. Austin picked up the list again and resisted the urge to sigh as he took in the next event. To his surprise, it was tomorrow. And a garden party. How different was that from a tea party?

With every second that went by, he was beginning to regret agreeing to any of this. Perhaps, if he played his cards right, he could make Miss Lavender regret it too.

***

The time for the garden party could not come quickly enough. Lavender was up from dawn, all but bouncing off the walls in her excitement. Not because of the event itself. She'd attended a garden party before and had found it dreadfully dull. There was no dancing and she had no interest in the games the ladies could play when they were not gossiping with each other.

But this party was different. The Countess of Lively would be in attendance. And Lavender would have an earl on her arm.

He wasn't the best option, she thought to herself when time finally came to prepare for the afternoon event. He was shabby, uncouth, irritable, and had such little social etiquette that it was a wonder he had been given the title in the first place. But he was an earl in the end. Attending the party on the arm of a titled gentleman was the first big step in executing her plan. She wouldn't let what happened yesterday affect today.

So she chose her gown carefully. A lovely primrose-colored gown with lace lining the neckline and the hems of her puffy sleeves. Her matching bonnet was settled over her perfectly styled hair. Her gloves and fan were simple enough to complement her attire without overshadowing it.

She'd detailed how Lord Derby was to dress for the event as well but she had little confidence that he would do it. It wasn't enough to lessen her excitement, though. She would simply make the best of what she was given. After all the time she'd spent preparing for this, she had no intention of letting this chance slip through her fingers.

For her father and his name, Lavender would see it through to the end.

She decided to take a carriage to Lord Derby's townhouse rather than ask him to come to her. A last minute alteration to her plan, but she didn't want to risk anything going wrong.

Thankfully, his townhouse wasn't far from hers. The carriage pulled up to a run-down house with a broken iron gate barring it from the street. Men came and went through the open front door, whom she assumed were there to work on the debilitated house. The paint was crumbling, the small garden overrun with weeds. The steps that led to the front porch were broken and the front door desperately needed to be replaced.

Lavender said nothing as she approached, silently drinking everything in. She spotted a man giving orders by the porch and waited for him to notice her. When he did, he quickly hurried over to her, bowing.

"Pardon the confusion," he said breathlessly. "You must be Miss Lavender. I am the butler of this house."

"Good day," Lavender greeted, smoothly stepping to the side as two men carted plywood into the house.

The butler looked visibly distressed by her sudden presence, which amused her a bit. "Please follow me, miss. I will inform Lord Derby of your arrival."

"Thank you," she murmured as she followed behind him, trying not to stare at the broken windowsill as she went by.

Inside the townhouse was no better. The foyer hummed with activity as men trudged back and forth, apparently under the watchful eye of the anxious butler. The carpet he brought her across was worn and frayed at the edges, barely hiding chips in the hardwood floor. A staircase greeted her on the other end of the foyer and Lavender breathed a sigh of relief when the butler took her past the creaking steps and to a nondescript door around the corner.

The butler gave her a hasty bow once inside. "Please make yourself comfortable, miss. Lord Derby will be with you shortly."

"Yes, thank you. Wait a moment."

The butler paused in expectation. Lavender pointed to the fading, peeling wallpaper of blue flowers. "Do you know what Lord Derby intends to do with the walls?"

The butler looked confused. "He has not said, miss. But the wallpaper is in desperate need of replacing."

"I agree. But perhaps you could find the same type?" Lavender smiled at him. "A simple suggestion, that's all."

"A-ah, yes, miss. I shall see to it. Please, excuse me."

Lavender gave him a small smile as she watched him leave, then turned to face the room.

What a...sight. She didn't know what to think of it. The entire townhouse was in desperate need of repairs, that was for certain. Everywhere she looked she spotted something broken, chipped, or worn.

She wandered over to one of the large bay windows washing the room in natural light. Of course, the paint was peeling from its surface. Lavender ran her finger over the sill, studying the lines sunken within.

"Do you make it a habit of arriving at other's residence without prior announcement?"

The grumble from behind sent her heart racing. Lavender let out a calming breath before turning to face him, a retort ripe on her tongue.

It died the moment she laid eyes on the earl. He looked...handsome. Not the rough handsomeness that had been hiding under layers of scowls and an unkempt attire. It was as if it had all been scrubbed away, revealing the gorgeous man underneath. His hair looked like it had been brushed and styled away from his face, with a healthy sheen that made it seem like he had washed it just this morning. His waistcoat was fitted to his body, the white shirt underneath molded to his muscular forearms. The bruises he'd sported yesterday had faded to a dull brown color.

It was like he had stepped right out of every lady's fantasy. One of her fantasies.

Even that ever present scowl was not enough to slow her racing heart. Goodness, what had gotten into her?

"Well?" the earl growled.

Lavender turned her back to him, taking a discreet deep breath. "I thought it would be best if I came to you, my lord," she explained, grateful that her voice sounded normal. "I did not want to leave it in your hands."

"How kind of you," he drawled. She listened to his approach and steeled herself. Something odd was happening in the pit of her stomach. Like a host of birds were swarming her insides. "Let us get this over with then."

Unable to help herself, Lavender risked looking at him. He was only two feet away from her, frowning out the window. "You look well put together, my lord," she said. "Perhaps a smile will be enough to complete it."

"I have no reason to smile. I have been dreading this from the moment you gave me that foolish list."

"You will thank me when we arrive at the party and no one will have any reason to speak badly about you."

He scoffed. "If you think they need a reason to do such a thing, you don't know the kind of people you're dealing with."

Fair enough. Her father had seen firsthand how damaging the wagging tongues of the tongue could be. And she was sure Lord Derby was no stranger to their harsh words.

"Forgive me," she murmured. "That was insensitive of me."

"Why? Because I am a bastard?"

"Yes," she replied without hesitation.

For a beat, the earl said nothing. Lavender was almost certain that she'd upset him further by being so blunt. Just as she was about to apologize, he exhaled sharply, the sound sounding suspiciously like a breathy laugh.

"For such a small lady," he said, "you certainly enjoy playing with fire."

"A small flame never hurt a soul before," Lavender said, giving him a small smile. He didn't smile back. But he didn't scowl either. He only stared at her without saying a word, eyes searching her face as if he were looking for something.

Lavender turned away, heat crawling up her neck. "You have a lovely home, my lord."

"Sarcasm does not become you," he drawled from behind.

She wandered over to the unlit hearth, staring up at the white molding lining the ceiling. "I speak the truth. Certainly, it is a little worse for wear but I can see the charm hidden beneath it all. What are the renovations you intend on doing?"

He didn't answer right away. After a few seconds of silence, she didn't think he would answer her at all. But then he said, "I am only going to repair all that are damaged. I have no intentions of changing anything."

"Good. I wouldn't want you to."

She sensed his surprise before she saw it. "You don't?"

"Of course not." Lavender ran her hand over the mantle. "You have a lovely home, my lord. And I can see the charm hidden underneath it all. I would hate for you to change the true character of this beautiful house."

"I...did not expect you to say that."

"Why?" Lavender raised a brow at him, a mirthful smile playing around her lips. "Did you think I would criticise every inch of this place?"

To her surprise, he hesitated before he nodded, "Yes."

Her mirth spilled over into true laughter. "Well, you needn't worry about that. This is your home, my lord. You can do whatever you wish with it. Even if I did not approve of your plan, you do not strike me as the type to care."

"I do not."

Lavender nodded. "But...if you did care, I hope you will not change those ornate bookshelves." She pointed to the other side of the room. "I adore them."

Lord Derby took in the bookshelves for a moment. He leaned against the bay window, crossing his arms. Lavender wondered if it was safe for the window to have such heavy weight pressed against it, considering its state.

"Those were a favourite of my mother's as well," he murmured so quietly that she almost didn't hear him.

"Your mother's...?" It took her a moment to remember. "Your mother was a maid, was she not?"

"She was."

"Was she—"

"We have a foolish party to attend, don't we?" He moved away from the window, stalking towards the door. "Let us get this over with then."

He didn't wait for her to respond before he left her staring after him.

Chapter Ten

Austin didn't think he would be back here. He'd even promised himself that he would never again set foot on this estate if he could help it. Had it not been for the lady sitting to his right, he wouldn't even be in this community at all.

The Pemberton House was just as populated as it was the last time Austin was there. It had been three years ago when his father had been on his deathbed. The ailing man had begged Austin to attend Lord Pemberton's evening ball in his stead, since he could not attend. Austin had only gone because of how his father had begged him at the time. And at first, it hadn't been bad. Other than the incessant gossiping of both ladies and gentlemen of the ton, he had nearly enjoyed himself. Locked up in the cards room with the other gentlemen who would much rather been drinking and playing cards than dancing, he'd begun to enjoy himself.

Until he'd gotten a little too inebriated and accused Lord Pemberton of cheating during their game of whist. The other man had gotten so mad that he'd banned him from the ball that evening.

Austin couldn't help but wonder if Lord Pemberton knew that he would be there this afternoon. He was looking forward to seeing the surprise on his face, if that were the case.

"We're here."

Austin looked down at Miss Lavender, wondering if she knew she had spoken aloud. The entire carriage ride had gone by in silence and the closer they came to Pemberton House, the more anxious she became. She couldn't hide it. Her leg shook, she picked at her nails, and she was nibbling on her bottom lip with such force that Austin was nearly certain she would soon draw blood.

As the carriage swung past the gates, she looked at him. "The Countess of Lively will be in attendance."

Ah, now it made sense.

"We cannot afford to make any mistakes," she went on. "The only aim for this afternoon is to engage in lighthearted conversation with a few people, stay polite, smile, and avoid her at all costs."

"Avoid her?" He frowned. "I thought you were trying to impress her."

"Yes, but flocking to her side is not the way to go. She will notice us the moment we arrive so the time will come in the future. For now, I just want to make sure we don't invite any scandal."

Miss Lavender looked back out the window, drawing in a breath when the carriage came to a stop.

"You're nervous," Austin pointed out.

"Yes, well you make me nervous," she shot back. He watched as she closed her eyes as if she was trying to calm herself. "I just...do not want a repeat of what happened at yesterday's party."

"I won't talk about my prizefighting then," he said without thinking.

She looked surprised at that, mimicking the emotion coursing through him. He didn't care, he told himself. It would only be easier on him if he didn't have to deal with the drama that came with such a confession.

"Thank you. I would appreciate that." She drew in a deep breath. "Well, shall we?"

Austin caught the hint, realizing she expected him to open the door for her. For the sake of peace, he alighted from the carriage and helped her exit. Her cheeks had lost some of its color but, he had to admit that she looked rather nice. Perhaps she was not as plain as he'd thought her to be. Did her hair always light up with golden streaks under the sunlight or was he imagining it?

He tucked her arm into him and she flashed him a relief smile that fell as quickly as it came. Together, they followed the footman who had appeared to lead them to the garden.

The party was already in full swing. Austin spotted Lord Pemberton instantly and did not miss the scowl that came over his face at the sight of him. Austin bit back his grin as the gentleman approached.

"Lord Derby," Lord Pemberton greeted. "I am surprised to see you here."

"Lord Pemberton," Austin responded. "As am I, in truth."

Lavender dug her fingers into his arm. "My lord," she greeted the host with a curtsy, putting on that sickly sweet voice she never used with Austin. "Thank you for your invitation. I have heard many things about your events so I am happy to be given the chance to experience it for myself."

Lord Pemberton's smile was a little more pleasant for Miss Lavender. "I am happy to have you here. Won't your brother be in attendance as well?"

"He had an important meeting to attend to, unfortunately. But I did not want for chaperones, you see."

"Yes, I do see." Lord Pemberton returned his attention to Austin, barely concealing his distaste. "I did not think that you two were acquainted."

"Do you know each other well?" Miss Lavender asked.

"Well enough," Austin said with a small smirk. "Say, my lord, would you care for another game of whist this afternoon?"

"I have other guests to attend to, I'm afraid," he pushed through gritted teeth. "But perhaps another time."

With that, he walked off. Austin chuckled to himself.

"What was that about?" the lady on his arm asked. He couldn't help but notice how perfectly she fit there. And she smelled wonderful, as usual

"Lord Pemberton and I do not like each other," Austin explained. "No, actually, he does not like me. I do not care about him."

"You seem to take much pleasure out of riling him though." She sighed softly as they made their way deeper into the party. Austin didn't miss the fact that everyone seemed to be staring at them. "It seems we are already off to a bad start."

"He did not kick us out. That is good enough, given his penchant for doing such things."

"Did he kick you out of his party before?" she asked with a small gasp.

"Let's just say that he is not very fond of being called a cheater."

Miss Lavender shook her head. "I do not know what surprises me more. The fact that you are not already making this afternoon difficult for me or the fact that you had attended a party before, given your hatred for the ton."

"I am a complex man, Miss Lavender."

"Lavender," she said. They stopped by the refreshments table and she picked up two glasses of lemonade, handing him one.

"Pardon?"

"Call me Lavender. I have been thinking about it and I think it will help if we refer to each other more familiarly. So call me Lavender and I shall call you Austin. How does that sound?"

"Not ideal."

"Lovely. Now put a smile on your face. Lady Lively is looking at us."

Austin began looking around to see for himself but Lavender tugged on his arm. "Don't look! We don't want too much of her attention, remember?"

"I remember," he grumbled. "Though that does not make any sense to me."

Lavender sighed, sipping her lemonade. "You do not have to understand it. Just go along with what I say and everything will go well."

He said nothing, studying the way her eyes skimmed over the garden, barely brushing over Lady Lively. It didn't make any sense. The countess she wanted to impress was right there and yet she wanted to ignore her? This was really important to her, it seemed. More important than he'd believed at first. This silly little quest to make it to the top of the upper class couldn't possibly be enough to make her this fearful.

But why? Because of her father? That couldn't be it.

He was tempted to question her about it again, even though he doubted she would give him a proper answer, but his chance disappeared when they were approached by two ladies. They greeted Lavender as if they'd known her forever and it didn't take him very long to realize that they were all friends.

To his relief, Lavender didn't seem very inclined to make him speak. She was clearly avoiding another situation like yesterday. So she took charge of every conversation they engaged in, all the while wearing that perfect mask that made her the spitting image of every other lady he'd ever seen. The woman who had been slumped in a couch groaning about how her plan was over had disappeared. The same woman who he'd found with ink all over her hands as she poured over the details of this plan was gone.

Perfect and ladylike Miss Lavender was the one by his side.

Austin didn't know whether to resent it or to admire it. All he knew was that it was working. More and more people seemed happy to speak with them, some even bold enough to comment on how proper she appeared considering the fact that she was not a titled lady. Lavender took it all with grace and left him very little chance to give his input.

He was so taken by her performance that the answer to his question didn't dawn on him until they were hours into the party.

Lavender was afraid of the Countess of Lively.

He saw it in the way she trembled when the countess was near, how she began tripping over her words if she was mentioned in conversation. It didn't look as if she was simply trying to play her cards right and make her move when she was ready. Austin was almost certain that she was terrified of actually making that move.

To test the theory, he made an attempt. To talk, to make suggestions that they move to shadier parts of the gardens. He even began a conversation with a group of gentlemen he did not like—Lord Pemberton included—because they were standing rather close to where Lady Lively sat with the younger ladies fussing over her.

"What are you doing?" Lavender asked him once they had a moment to themselves.

"What do you mean? I am playing along, like you asked me to."

"Yes, and that is suspicious enough." She narrowed her eyes at him. It was far more adorable than threatening, Austin thought. "What are you up to?"

"Nothing at all." Then he saw his chance. Lady Lively had left her table and was making her way over to them. If Lavender saw her, she would bolt. So he put a hand on her shoulder, hoping it would keep her attention on him.

All it did was make her more suspicious. She didn't pull away but she tilted her head to the side as if she was trying to understand his aim.

"What are you looking at?" she asked, attempting to turn around.

"You," he said quickly. The hand on her shoulder wasn't enough. So he brushed his knuckles along her jawline in a far more tender motion than he'd intended.

They both froze. Her eyes went wide, lips parting in shock. Austin never noticed how perfectly they were shaped, her bottom lip slightly fuller than the top. They were the same color as the blush staining her cheeks.

He didn't remember about the countess making her way to them. Couldn't remember why he had begun doing this in the first place. All he could think was that the gold flecks in her eyes must not have been there when they first met, because how didn't he notice it before?

"Miss Lavender Latrice."

The countess' voice broke the suspended moment. Lavender gasped quietly, eyes filling bewilderment then betrayal when she realized what he'd done. He watched the mask fall over her face once more before she turned to face the countess.

"Lady Lively." Lavender curtsied. "It is good to see you again."

Again?

Lady Lively looked exactly how Austin imagined her. An aging lady with judgmental eyes, thin lips, and graying hair. She didn't bother to hide the fact that she was looking both Lavender and Austin up and down.

"Yes, I did not expect to see you in such a social setting again," she responded at last. "And with the Earl of Derby with you as well."

"Life has quite a way of throwing surprises at you, doesn't it?" Lavender said with a soft chuckle. Austin could almost believe that she was not nervous at all.

"It does, it does. But a garden party, Miss Lavender? Hopefully you have learned your lesson after the last one."

Lavender's smile faltered for a second. "You needn't worry, my lady."

"Me? Worried?" The countess laughed behind her fan. "I won't do such a thing. It is Lord Derby who should be worried. Or perhaps you two are fit for each other, considering his reputation as well."

Austin was already regretting his plan to force them to interact. "Choice words, my lady," he said, keeping his voice as civil as he could. "Though rather bold considering you value propriety. I would hate for you to make a fool of yourself."

Lady Lively was far better at keeping her mask in place than Lavender was. "Oh, heavens, my lord. I was only making reference to something that happened in the past. You see, Miss Lavender, made the silly mistake of telling a gentleman that he had torn a hole in his breeches during a game of croquette when she was last invited to a garden party. You and I both know that it is not becoming of a lady."

His irritation shot to the sun. "And you, *countess*—"

"I appreciate your concern for me, my lady," Lavender cut in. "I won't make such a silly mistake again."

"I would hope not. Honestly, I had wondered who would want someone who would make such a comment. But seeing you with the Earl of Derby…"

Austin was used to hearing such things about him. Perhaps not to his face but he didn't put anything past judgmental ladies who thought they were above everyone else. Had he been alone, he would have ignored her. Or perhaps left a scathing remark that would show her just how ungentlemanly he could be.

But Lavender spoke before he could. "Austin was kind enough to accept me as his betrothed, my lady. It is me who should be grateful to him."

"Certainly, certainly. A rowdy man like the earl is more suited to your tastes after all."

"Yes, of course." Her voice was quiet. "Please pardon me."

Without waiting for a response, Lavender ducked her head and walked away in the direction of the house, leaving Austin with the sick feeling that he might have made a mistake.

Chapter Eleven

At some point, she couldn't see where she was going. The tears that blurred her eyes didn't seem ready to fall just yet, waiting for her to be safely locked away where no one could see her. She headed straight for the powder room, after receiving directions on how to find it from a maid. Locked within, everything came pouring out.

Lady Lively was just as ruthless as she remembered her to be. The worst thing was that the countess knew that she was untouchable, so much so that she could say whatever she wanted without receiving any backlash. No one would ever dare say such scathing remarks directly to someone else's face. And yet the Countess of Lively did not hesitate. She'd gone out of her way, approached her directly, to reduce Lavender to the dirt under her shoe.

Austin had seen it all. He'd watched the countess approaching and hadn't said a word about it even though he knew Lavender was avoiding her. Was that the reason he had touched her so tenderly? God, how could she have fallen for that?

Lavender held in her sobs as the tears ran down her face in rivulets. She wouldn't dare allow anyone to see or hear her cry. But no matter how hard she tried to stop, the tears kept coming. She didn't know how long she spent in there.

I have to follow through with this. I won't allow her to stop me.

Lady Lively was right about many things. Lavender's improper words at the last garden party, even though she had been trying to save the gentleman from embarrassment by pointing it out to him. Lord Derby's rough demeanour that was quite unbecoming of proper earl. And yes, perhaps on the outside it looked as if they were perfect for each other.

But she was more than her title—or lack thereof. At the end of that, everyone would know. She just had to keep going.

At last, the tears abated. Lavender wiped away what was left of it and pulled her shoulders back. She had to get back out there and put that smile back on her face, no matter how false it was.

As soon as she stepped out of the powder room, a large shadow fell over her. Lavender gasped when she saw that it was Austin.

"What are you doing?" she cried. "Don't you know how improper it is for you to be so close to a ladies' powder room?"

Austin scoffed. "You people and your rules," he grumbled and grasped her hand. "Come. We're leaving."

"Leaving? What do you mean, we're leaving?"

"Just that." He pulled her down a path that would lead them back to the carriage. "We have no reason to be here any longer."

"But we can't just leave," she protested. "We have to at least say goodbye to the host."

"They will figure it out eventually."

"But—"

"Do you want to stay?" he asked, stopping abruptly to face her. "After everything that had just been said to you, I thought you would jump at the thought of returning home."

"I..." She was having a hard time wrapping her mind around what was happening. "You're leaving because of me?"

"I don't particularly enjoy being here either," he grumbled.

Lavender didn't know what to say. All of a sudden, she realized how red her eyes had to be after her crying but Austin said nothing about it. How long had he been standing outside the powder room waiting for her to finish crying?

"I can't leave," she said at last. "I want to, but I have never been a coward and I won't start now. I won't let Lady Lively believe that she chased me away."

He only stared at her for a moment. If she didn't know better she would think that the look in his eyes was one of admiration.

"Very well," he conceded at last. "But if you insist on returning to the party then you should at least wipe your face properly."

He fished out a handkerchief from his waistcoat and handed it to her. Lavender gratefully accepted. "Thank you. And thank you for trying to rectify the situation you've caused. Don't think I didn't know that you were aware of Lady Lively approaching us."

"I was. And I said nothing because I was curious."

"About what?"

"About why you were so afraid of her. Now I know."

She let out a humorless laugh, handing him his handkerchief. "Then you understand me."

"What I don't understand is why you are going to such lengths to befriend someone like her. And there are dozens more lords and ladies just like the Countess of Lively. Why would you want to be a part of a society that would speak to you that way."

Lavender shook her head, heading back towards the party. The closer they drew to the sound of chatter, the more uncomfortable she became. But she hid it well. Hopefully.

"You won't understand," she deflected.

"Then help me understand," Austin pressed. "Especially if you want me to help you on this silly quest."

Lavender didn't respond. She didn't need to get into the whys of her questions right now. She just needed to make it to the end of the party without breaking down in tears again.

Thankfully, Austin didn't press her with any more questions. When they were within eyesight again, Lavender could tell everyone was talking about her. At least it felt that way. She was certain that the laughter coming from the table Lady Lively sat at was at her expense, though so she stayed away from it.

"They're staring at me, not you," Austin said.

Lavender frowned up at him. "Why would you think that?"

"No one heard the conversation you had with the countess," he said, tucking his hands in this pockets. He stared out at the guests as if he was displeased with every single one of them. "But they know who I am. The bastard earl. Everywhere I go they talk, and they watch me. So there's no need for you to think that you're the object of their stares."

Lavender blinked. "If I didn't know any better, I would think that you are trying to make me feel better."

"Then it is good that you do know better," he drawled.

Lavender laughed, surprising herself at how genuine it was. "We do make quite the pair, don't we?"

"The bastard earl and the sister of a wealthy merchant? Perhaps not as much as you think."

"Do you truly not realise how accepted you are by these people compared to me? Wealth or no, having no title is all that matters to them."

"Enough of them." He put his hand on the small of her back. Lavender stiffened as electric jolts raced up her spine. He began steering her towards the lords and ladies playing croquette. "We've done enough socialising for the afternoon. Let's spend the rest of our time here watching the croquette game."

"That...does not sound so bad."

"You will enjoy it immensely, I'm sure." He picked up two glasses of lemonade on the way there. Lavender felt cold without his touch. They chose an unoccupied table and he even pulled her chair out for her. "And don't worry. I will take on the hardship of informing anyone if their pants need mending."

Lavender tilted her head back and laughed.

***

He didn't believe the party would ever end. Austin trudged up the steps of his townhouse, noting that they had been fixed since leaving earlier this afternoon. Lavender was on her way home and he was free to resent this entire ordeal until the next event he was forced to attend.

Though, he supposed it wasn't that bad by the end of it. As soon as Lavender decided to ignore the guests and enjoy herself, Austin had seen her mask slip more than once. He realized he didn't mind the mask-less lady half as much. At least, not when they were laughing at the croquette players and gorging on lemonade.

He was not looking forward to the next event however. It had only been a few days and he was exhausted. Putting so much effort into his appearance for the party had been tiring on its own, even though it made him feel better about himself. All the effort had basically been for naught because of the drama surrounding Lavender and Lady Lively.

He still didn't understand why she was so determined to impress her after seeing what a horrible person the countess was. And he was too tired to care right now. He dragged himself through the foyer and to the closest drawing room, needing a drink.

The moment he stepped inside, he paused. The room looked...different. He couldn't tell how. The furniture was all in the same place. The bookshelves he'd asked the workmen not to touch hadn't moved from their spots.

It was the wallpaper, he realized. It was the same but different. Cleaner, no tears, bright. Had they been replaced?

"My lord." Right on time, his butler appeared. "I did not know you had returned home."

"Who did this?" Austin asked, wandering over to the nearest wall. He brushed his fingers against it, marveling at how smooth it was.

"The wallpaper, my lord?" The butler sounded confused. "The workmen took care of it while you were gone. I ensured that everything was put back in its rightful place before you returned home."

"Was it your idea?" Austin asked, looking back at it. "Replacing the wallpaper with exactly the same one?"

"No, my lord." The butler seemed anxious. "Miss Lavender made the suggestion when she visited this afternoon. I thought that it would be good to pay the suggestion heed seeing that she will soon become the lady of this house."

"Lavender did this?" he murmured to himself.

"Y-yes, my lord. Was it a mistake?"

"No." Austin cleared his throat. "You may go. Thank you."

"Very well, my lord." The butler all but scampered away.

Austin made his way to the sideboard and poured himself a much needed glass of scotch. How did she know about the wallpaper? He'd been so caught up in this betrothal and all that was expected of him that he'd forgotten to tell the workmen to leave the wallpaper be. His mother had loved it. And because she had, he loved it too.

How had she known?

No, she didn't know, he told himself. She didn't know a thing about him, other than the fact that he was a bastard, and yet she'd made such an important decision such as this.

Perhaps Lady Lively was right about one thing. Even though theirs was far from a love match, perhaps they were good for each other.

Chapter Twelve

"My dear sister, it has been far too long since I have seen you resting."

Lavender looked up at Vincent as he approached, lowering her book to her lap. "What exactly do you mean by that?"

He sank into the couch next to her, slinging his arm along the back of it. "You are usually doing something, these days. Writing in that little book of yours, planning something. Going from event to event."

"Oh heavens it has only been a few days. Otherwise, I am usually here in the library with my nose buried in a book. Which you are interrupting by the way."

Vincent laughed. When she attempted to ignore him by lifting her book again, he took it from her hands.

"How is Lord Derby?" he asked.

Lavender kept her face impassive even though her heart skipped a beat. She didn't know how to answer that. After they'd parted ways yesterday, things had felt different between them. Less like she was forcing a horse to drink water and more like the horse was fine with taking a few sips now and again. She couldn't fathom the thought that they'd bonded over the horrible interaction with Lady Lively.

Because she didn't know how to explain any of that to her brother, she said, "He is the Earl of Derby. The very same man I met that day."

"I see. That bad?" Vincent chuckled to himself. "Perhaps you two need to spend more time with each other then."

Lavender snatched the book from him and pretended to refocus her attention on the pages, even though the only thing she could think about now was the earl. "We spent the last two days together, however unwillingly. There's no need for me to see him again until the next time I need him."

"That is no way to treat your betrothed, Lavender," he chastised lightly.

"Oh, you and I both know that our marriage is one of convenience, Vincent."

"What is the status of his house's renovations then? Perhaps it would be nice for you to give it a woman's touch."

She sighed, closing her book. "You seem quite determined to get me out of the house, don't you?"

"Am I being obvious?" her brother asked with a cheeky grin.

Lavender rolled her eyes at him, getting to her feet. "Very well. I shall check in on the status of the workers and then return home. I shall be back within the hour."

"You may take more time—"

"Before the hour," she repeated on her way out the door.

Once she was in bedchamber, Lavender picked up the pace. She didn't pay that tremor of excitement any mind. She wasn't excited to see the earl at all. It would only be good to get out of the house for a while, to get some fresh air. That was the only reason why she'd chosen one of her favorite walking dresses with her matching bonnet and parasol.

Her brother called for a carriage to be prepared so it was ready for her by the time she made it outside. Betty seemed to be in a good mood as well, as if she was also looking forward to leaving the house as Lavender's chaperone.

Before long, they arrived at the house. It was in markedly better condition than yesterday, she noted. The front porch and window had been fixed. And there seemed to be twice as many workmen trudging in and out than there had been before. Perhaps Austin was getting impatient regarding the speed of the repairs.

"Miss Lavender!" The anxious butler came rushing up to her with sweat dotting his forward. "I did not know that you were—"

"Don't worry," she told him. "I did not send word that I would be coming. Is Lord Derby here?"

"He is not, miss. He stepped out just a short while ago and did not say where he was going."

"Did he take a carriage?"

"No, miss. He left on foot."

Perhaps that meant that he would not be gone for long. Not that she cared overly much. She'd come here to check on the renovations after all.

She said as much to the butler and he nodded eagerly. "I could take you on a tour through the house, miss, if you wish."

"That would be nice. You can also tell me what changes you intend on making as we go along."

"Certainly, miss."

Lavender followed the butler inside. He took Betty and her to the drawing room first, showing her that the wallpaper had been replaced like she'd suggested. Lavender felt a bite of pleasure when he said that Austin had seemed pleased by the sight of it.

The next room was a parlor. And then a sun-room. All rooms clearly had not been touched by the workmen yet because there were little repairs done to the dilapidated states, but the butler informed her of the plans for each room, which left her with hope.

Then they came to the dining room. The first thing she noticed was the large portrait hanging over the mantle across the room. Lavender hadn't noticed the lack of portraits in the house until she spotted this one.

A pair of deep blue eyes watched her from across the room. The woman in the portrait was a subtle beauty, bearing a small, kind smile. Lavender had a suspicion of who she was even as she asked, "Who is she?"

"She is the late Countess of Derby, miss," the butler responded.

"Is her portrait the only one in the house?"

"Yes, miss."

"How...sad."

"P-pardon me, miss?" The butler sounded taken aback.

Lavender drew closer, admiring the soft brushstrokes despite how sad she found it. "There is a certain emptiness to having this portrait as the only one in the house," she said. She heard something behind her but didn't turn to look, clasping her hands behind her instead. "I had heard that the late countess had borne no ill will to the earl and Austin but it is still quite sad to see that neither is displayed throughout the entire house. Perhaps I could speak with Austin about it when I see him next."

"Miss Lavender..." came Betty's soft whisper.

"Or is that a bad idea? He doesn't think very highly of me. He may think I am being nosy."

"Miss Lavender," her chaperone's voice came again. "Perhaps—"

"What is it, Betty?" Lavender turned to look at her. Only to find that it wasn't Betty standing slightly behind her but Austin.

How hadn't she heard him come in? The butler was nowhere to be found. Lavender wouldn't be surprised if he had run off the moment his master appeared. Betty was standing a few paces away, a fearful look on her face.

Lavender turned to face him, ignoring the rapid pounding of her heart. "You are quieter than you look," she commented.

To her slight relief, he didn't look as annoyed as he usually did. He crossed his arms and said, "So I have been told before. What are you doing here?"

"Can't a lady visit her betrothed?" she asked. He only raised a brow and she sighed. "I came to check on the renovations. Well, Vincent urged me to."

"I see." He came closer, stopping when he was right beside her. "And you think that my house is sad and empty because there is only one portrait displayed?"

"It may sound quite rude of me to say—"

"Which comes as no surprise to me," he cut in.

Lavender rolled her eyes. "But," she went on. "I stand by what I said. Wouldn't it be nice to have your portrait displayed as well? Or perhaps that of your mother's? Both?"

"Surely you do not think it appropriate to display my father's mistress? What would you think if you were to walk into a room and see such a thing?"

"Not every room needs to be open to the public," Lavender responded easily. "If it is the judgment of others that worries you, which is quite surprising, then you may hang the portrait someplace private."

Austin regarded her for a moment. "You are quite unusual. Do you know that?"

"I have been told," she said with a smile. "Why don't we take a break from all this talk of houses and portraits and go for a promenade in the park?"

"I cannot think of anything worse," he grumbled.

"Marvelous," Lavender quipped with a smile. She turned to the door. "I shall wait for you in the carriage while you fetch a coat."

Austin didn't make any more protests to the matter, to Lavender's surprise and relief. She was free to traipse out of the room in far better spirits than she had been when she'd arrived.

Odd.

**

"I hate this. I hate every second of this."

"Which is quite interesting considering how good you are at it." Lavender couldn't help her mirthful response. She was in too good of a mood to be bothered by Austin's grumpiness.

After all, she'd managed to drag him out of the house to Hyde Park and they were now walking arm in arm down a well-traveled path under the curious stares of others nearby. It wasn't the first time they were doing this and yet this time felt different. She didn't care so much about what others were thinking as they watched them as she did simply relaxing and enjoying herself.

Relaxing and enjoying herself around the Earl of Derby had once seemed impossible.

"Why are there so many people here," he continued to grumble. "I thought these people were important members of society. Don't they have more important things to do than walk about a park?"

"They are likely here for the same reason we are," Lavender responded lightly. "To relax and enjoy nature with their peers."

"That doesn't sound like what we are doing. You are here to put on a show for your quest and I am here because I have no choice."

"How odd. Surely you aren't admitting that a small helpless lady like me forced you into doing something you do not wish to do?"

Austin looked at her and Lavender met his eyes with a cheeky grin. "You are getting far too comfortable if you think it is a good idea to jest with me," he mumbled.

"You will do me no harm. Perhaps you have even grown fond of me."

"That assertion appears rather exaggerated."

Lavender just laughed. She wouldn't forget the fact that he had waited for her outside the powder room and had been ready to take her home. She wouldn't forget the attempts he'd made to make her forget about what Lady Lively had said. Honestly, Lavender didn't think she *could* forget. Perhaps that was the reason she was more than fine with being here with him rather than locked away in the library like she usually was.

"I know you are only here to put on a performance, Lavender," Austin spoke again.

There was just something about the way he said her name that did something to her. Something she could not define just yet. "Of course I am. We are already here. We might as well continue our charade of acting like a loving couple."

"Even though it is clear as day that our betrothal is an arranged one," he pointed out.

"Well, perhaps it would not be so clear if you did not wear that frown all the time." Lavender reached up and pressed a finger in the center of his forehead. It succeeded in getting him to relax. "See? Already better."

"I like my frown. It keeps people away."

"No one will dare approach you with or without it," she assured. "And while we are at it, why don't you straighten your back a bit more?"

His frown returned with full force. "Straighten my back? It is straight enough."

"Not nearly so," she told him. She put a hand on his back and forced his chest out. Lavender bit her lip to hold in her laughter as she cupped his chin, forcing his head up and slowed her walk so that he was forced to walk slower as well.

It took Austin a few seconds to realize that she was poking fun at him. He relaxed, growling, "You think you are quite funny, don't you?"

"I am the most hilarious person I know. And if you would simply relax, perhaps you would know that as well."

"I cannot do so knowing that at any moment you will spring another sordid event on me and force me to attend with you."

"It won't be 'at any moment'," she corrected. "We have someplace else to attend in the next week."

"Next few days?" He paused, clearly thinking. "I thought I would have two weeks' break before we are to attend that ball of yours."

"That ball of mine is Lady Henley's masquerade ball and I worked very hard to secure an invitation. But no, I have modified the list of events I gave to you." Lavender caught his look of horror and couldn't help but laugh. "I thought it was a little unfair to only attend places I wanted to go to, so I added a few sporting events as well."

"You did?" He seemed incredulous.

"Not only for your sake, I assure you. A number of people from the ton attend such events so it will aid in my plan all the same. But I thought that perhaps you would be less likely to complain the entire time if you were enjoying yourself a little." She paused to frown at him. "You are a lover of sports, aren't you?"

"It depends. What kind are you talking about?"

"The next will be a horse racing event. I added a fencing match as well."

"Horse racing, you say." His distrusting expression faded into something quite close to satisfaction. "That does not sound too bad."

"Wonderful. I hoped you would say as much."

His scowl returned, though with markedly less force. "I hope you are not waiting for me to thank you."

Lavender shook her head with a smile. "I know better than to expect such a thing."

"Good."

Silence fell between them. Lavender kept that cheeky smile on her face, waiting for Austin to realize that that wasn't the end of it.

After a few seconds, he narrowed his eyes at her. "What is it? Why are you smiling like that?"

"Have I told you how handsome you looked yesterday, my lord?" she asked in an overly kind voice.

"Out with it. Your addition of the sporting events comes with a clause, doesn't it?"

"How astute of you. The answer is yes. It is dependent on you attending the tailor alongside me and my brother in a few days."

"The answer is no."

"May I remind you of what you're giving up?" she probed. They came to a stop by a pond. Lavender pulled her arm free of his and turned her back to the quacking ducklings to smile up at him. "Horses. Racing. Shouting. The hot sun." She paused. "Remind me again why men enjoy such things?"

Laughter shot past his lips before he could stop it. Lavender's eyes lit up with similar mirth. "You're a persistent lady, you know," he said.

"I am well aware. So, do we have a deal?"

"Reluctantly."

"Marvelous!" She slid her arm through his once more. "Now let us walk around some more to show these fickle lords and ladies what a lovely match we are."

Oddly enough, Austin didn't mind the thought of that half as much.

Chapter Thirteen

"Please forgive the intrusion, my lord, but this is a matter that needs your prompt attention."

Austin turned to look at his butler with a raised brow. The firm tone he'd heard just now turned into a bumbling mess the moment Austin's eyes fell on him. His butler backed into the threshold of the study and bowed deeply.

"If it pleases you, my lord."

Austin only stared at him for a long moment. Then he chuckled under his breath. He saw the moment his butler stiffened at the sound, as if he was bracing for something horrible.

Once upon a time, the servants had only been apprehensive of him. They'd stayed out of his way, treating him with the respect that should be given to the earl's son—bastard or no—but never truly interacting with him. That apprehension shot up to true fear the day Austin received the title and he'd been fine with it. He didn't care if the housekeeper and the maids avoided him as if he were the plague. And it didn't matter to him that his butler shook in his boots every time he had to interact with him.

For some reason, watching a grown man tremble in fear when he was only doing his job, made him uncomfortable. Austin could only laugh at himself. Since when had he cared? And why did it bother him so much so suddenly?

"What is it?" he asked in as calm a voice as he could muster. He'd retreated to his study after breakfast wanting to stay out of the way of the workmen and find some solitude so he hoped this conversation would not be long.

The butler straightened and licked his lips, visibly wiping the trepidation from his face. "Your steward sends word from the main estate, my lord. I believe there are certain matters that require your attention, ones he cannot undertake in your stead."

Austin looked down at the bound book and what looked like a letter in the butler's hand. "And I assume that is from him?"

"Yes, my lord. He says that it is a matter of urgency."

"Hm." Austin turned to the window. "Put it on my desk."

"Yes, my lord."

He listened to the butler's quick footsteps behind him as he hurried to do as he was told. Before he could leave, Austin said, "You have been employed by my father for a while now, haven't you?"

"Y-yes, my lord. I have been the butler of this townhouse for fifteen years."

"Fifteen years. That is long enough to watch me grow up, though I admittedly did not spend much time in London."

"I suppose, my lord."

Austin turned at the uncertainty in the butler's voice. He didn't know why he was doing this. He didn't care to know his servants better. The last thing he wanted to do was embrace this life that had been forced onto him, rather than accepted willingly.

But there was a certain brown-eyed lady floating around in his mind since his walk through the park yesterday and it was making him feel...nice. He was in an unusually good mood, even though there was the looming task of going to the tailor in his near future. Perhaps that was the reason he didn't feel instant annoyance at his butler interrupting his alone time.

"What is your name?" Austin asked, leaning on the wide windowsill. "I realise I have never asked you before."

The butler looked startled. "My name?" It is Mr. Jonathan Francis, my lord."

"Mr. Francis." Austin hoped he could remember that. He had a feeling this wasn't the first time he'd been told. "Thank you for your assistance, Mr. Francis."

The butler looked at a loss for words. Austin gave him a few seconds to come to terms with what he'd just said, and then he told him, "You may leave now."

"Yes, my lord." Mr. Francis left slower than he usually did, as if he were in a daze.

Odd of him to care about such a thing, Austin thought as he made his way to his desk. He only knew the name of the butler at the main estate, where he had spent most of his time. And that man was no more comfortable with him as Mr. Francis was.

Austin reached for the letter first, skimming through it out of mere curiosity. It was certainly a serious matter. Apparently, there were a number of servant posts now vacant at the estate since quite a few of the maids and footmen resigned. The other estates within the earldom also required considerable attention that his steward could not give himself. The bound book, Austin realized, was a ledger book. One quick look through it told him that things were not looking good.

He had been pouring all of his attention into the repairs that he hadn't given a single thought to anything else. And that was on purpose. Austin hadn't wanted this title. He didn't want the responsibility that came with managing so many things at once. Just looking at this ledger book brought on a slight megrim.

He tossed the book onto the desk and rubbed his temple. What should he do now? For a while now, he'd been content to ignore all his responsibilities, to do the bare minimum that was expected of him. But he'd known deep down that it wouldn't be long before everything he was running from caught up to him. And he wasn't prepared for it.

Austin didn't know how long he sat there pondering his life's decisions when there was another knock on the door.

"Come," he called gruffly, a little grateful for the distraction.

He expected it to be Mr. Francis, back to bother him with another annoying decision he had to make as earl. When Lavender slipped into the study instead, Austin almost couldn't believe his eyes.

She didn't look at him first. Her eyes ran around the room, drinking in every inch of his study. Austin felt a tremor of anxiousness as she took everything in. The study was the last room to be renovated since he'd needed a place where he could disappear from everything else while the repairs were underway. He hadn't expected to have anyone else in here but him.

What did she think of this place? Was she judging him for letting it get this bad?

Austin didn't say anything, watching as she made her way to the center of the room. He didn't realize he was holding his breath until she turned to him with no judgment in her eyes.

"I see why you spend so much time in here," she said. "I would too, but with perhaps a book or two."

Austin leaned back in his chair, relief flooding him like a tidal wave. He didn't like the feeling. He hadn't cared about what others thought of him before so what did her opinion matter?

"I am not a lover of books," he told her. "I much prefer drinking and brooding."

"That does not surprise me in the slightest." She wandered closer, sinking into the chair across from his desk. A smile was playing around her lips. She looked well put together as usual, no different from the daughters and wives of wealthy lords. Her hair, however, had been left down around her shoulders in natural waves. It made her face look softer, her eyes rounder, her lips fuller. Or had she always looked like that?

"What are you doing here, Lavender?" he asked her.

"I am here to pay you a visit."

"Is it not customary to send word of your visit beforehand?"

"I have never done so before," she said with a shrug. "Why should I begin now?"

Austin held back his smirk. That was certainly true. "Please tell me you aren't here to drag me to the park again. I have not recovered from your last two attempts."

"Successful attempts, I must add." She didn't care to hide her smile. It tugged at her cheeks in such full force that her entire face shone like the sun. "But no, that isn't why I have decided to grace you with my presence on this fine afternoon."

"The tailor?" Austin asked, a little apprehensive.

"No, no. However, please note that the appointment is already set."

"Already?" He couldn't help the scowl that overtook his face. It came as natural to him as breathing but instead of returning the scowl like she usually did, she laughed.

"Yes, but as I said, that isn't the reason I have come. I was thinking about the garden party and our interaction with Lady Lively."

Austin searched her face for a moment. He saw no signs of her previous anxiousness. "What about it?"

"As you know, Lady Lively is the epitome of ladylike—"

"I know no such thing."

Lavender rolled her eyes and folded her arms. "And you, my lord, are nothing of the sort. You are so far from what a proper lord should be that I wonder if you will be helpful or damaging to my plan."

Austin felt a sharp pang of annoyance at those words. So she hadn't come here for any other reason that for her own foolish plan.

"I'm sorry to tell you, Lavender," he said in a tone that implied he wasn't sorry at all. "But I am who I am. You cannot take the bastard out of the man."

"That is nonsense and you know it. I have heard many rumours about you, Austin."

"From your maid."

She smiled brightly at that and Austin's scowl grew deeper. "Yes, that is right. And she tells me that you were accepted by your father from birth. You grew along sons of other lords and were given the highest possible education men of your stature can receive. I have no doubt that you have what it takes to become a true and proper earl."

"And what if I don't want to be?" Austin asked with a raised brow. He ignored the irony of the situation, considering his confusion earlier while looking through the ledger book.

"You have no choice in the matter."

Lavender was in a chipper mood, he realized. Despite his grumpiness, she faced him with nothing but bright words and a smile on her face. Lavender pulled her chair towards the desk until she was close enough to rest her elbows on top.

"Now, pretend that I am Lady Lively," she said. "And I have approached you at the horse racing match. How will you greet me?"

Austin just stared at her. Lavender's smile began to slip as her expectancy morphed into curiosity then confusion.

"Don't you know what to say?" she asked at last.

"You asked, how will I greet her. I do not intend on greeting the countess at all."

"Goodness, you are being quite stubborn, aren't you?" She shifted in the chair. Austin realized after a moment that she was tucking her legs underneath her. "Very well, how about this? What will you say if someone were to ask about your feelings towards your betrothed?"

"Why is that anyone's business?"

"It does not matter. They will ask regardless."

Austin couldn't deny that. The ton were a nosy bunch.

He considered the question for a moment. His first inclination would be to tell them the truth and not care about what they thought of it. It took him a moment to realize that he didn't quite know what the truth was.

He'd resented Lavender for a moment when they'd first met, even though he'd walked into this betrothal himself. For making him do the things he'd always dreaded, for dragging him around as if he were nothing but a prop in her play. But now, none of that remained.

Right now when he looked at her, he felt…something. It was potent, rearing its ugly head every time he looked directly into her eyes. But he didn't know what that something was. All he knew was that he didn't feel any irritation when she'd walked into the room. And when she'd scooted her chair closer, a part of him wished that she would bring it to his side of the desk instead.

"She is my betrothed," he said at last when he realized that she was still waiting for his response.

"That…" Lavender frowned, looking disappointed. "That is not a proper response at all."

Austin only shrugged.

For the first time since she'd walked into the room, she looked genuinely frustrated. Suddenly, she began getting to her feet even though she'd only just gotten comfortable.

"Come with me," she said.

"Where? Why?"

"There is a garden behind this house, is there not? Let us go for a walk. Get some fresh air."

Austin found himself standing without realizing it. "Oh, dear, this woman and her walks," he grumbled loud enough for her to hear.

Lavender laughed and turned away before she caught the end of a smile he'd been trying to hide.

Chapter Fourteen

Lavender didn't know what possessed her to leave her comfortable house to come and visit Austin but she didn't question it at all. But she supposed that coming here under the guise of teaching him how to be more gentlemanly was a good excuse as any. He didn't need to know that she was really just looking forward to spending time with him.

How quickly things changed.

Lavender couldn't help glancing at him as they strolled between the surprisingly manicured rows of bushes in his garden. She'd expected the garden to be in as much a sorry state as the townhouse. But, even though she spotted a few overgrown areas, Lavender supposed it was easier to care for the landscape than it was to care for a building.

He didn't notice her stares. Or at least, she hoped he didn't. She wouldn't know how to explain herself if he did. How would she be able to tell him that she didn't quite understand why she felt so at peace, why she was so fine with them strolling in silence rather than charging headfirst into preparations for her plan like she had been since they'd met? Lavender couldn't understand it herself. He was a handsome man, undoubtedly. And his grumpiness had an underlying layer of charm that many others wouldn't see.

But beyond that, Lavender was beginning to realize that she liked him. Perhaps they could be friends after all of this.

"Will you say something or do you intend for us to make laps around the garden until you have found your tongue?"

Even his gruff words did not inspire any annoyance in her like they usually did. Lavender only laughed. She'd been laughing and smiling ever since she arrived. Maybe she was just in an exceptional mood today.

"Goodness, can't a woman enjoy the beautiful weather before she has to face the task of forcing you into submission?"

"Ah, so you are aware of the fact that you are forcing me then."

"Well...forcing, cajoling, convincing. These are all words we can use."

"I doubt it. You are like a bull intent on knocking down everything in your path."

"Oh, Austin, that is the nicest thing you have ever said to me," Lavender sang. She looked up at him just in time to catch the end of a smile before he smothered it under his usual scowl.

"Except the Countess of Lively," he pointed out.

Lavender didn't rise to the bait. She knew it was coming. Her shoddy performance at Lord Pemberton's garden party had been enough to raise questions Lavender wasn't prepared to answer just yet. She was surprised it had taken him this long.

"I suppose," she answered mildly. "But it shan't happen again."

"Why did it happen in the first place?" he persisted, much to her surprise. "You spoke so confidently about your plan to overthrow Lady Lively that I could not believe how fearful you were to speak to her."

"I was not fearful," she defended. "I was biding my time. And the garden party wasn't the right time."

"That wasn't what it was and you know it." They came to a small bench. Austin chose to sit so Lavender did the same. "You were basically shaking when she was approaching you."

"When she snuck up on me, you mean. Don't think I have forgotten about the fact that you knew she was walking up to us."

"Because I wanted to see how you would respond. And it was not well."

Lavender rolled her eyes. "How astute of you, my lord. And here I thought you didn't care about my plan."

"I do not. It doesn't mean I am not curious."

"If you wish to know so badly then you should answer a few questions of my own."

"I pass," he said without hesitation and began to rise.

"Wait!" Lavender grabbed his arm with both her hands. She hadn't paid much attention to how muscular his forearm was until she felt it herself. He tensed at her touch but didn't pull away, only looking down at her. "Come now, don't run. Sit, sit."

She patted the spot he had just vacated and try to ignore the flutter of her heart when he looked down at her hands. Lavender took her time in letting him go. She thought he would just walk away and leave her there so her surprise overcame her slight nervousness when he sat down instead.

"Out with it then," he grunted.

Lavender folded her hands in her lap. Her gaze fell on his own hands. She hadn't forgotten the way it felt when those large hands had brushed against her cheek at the garden party. Now she knew that he'd done it to distract her. And distract her it had. So easily, so thoroughly that she had gone to bed the same night thinking about that simple touch.

"Why do you do prizefighting?" she asked at last.

Austin drew in a slow breath, staring out ahead of him. "Because I like it."

"I'm sure there is more to it than that. How did you get into it in the first place?"

"It just happened."

"You are being purposely vague," she said with a pout.

"And you are being annoyingly insistent."

"Can you blame me? It is such an unusual thing for a man like yourself that I cannot help but be curious." Lavender paused for a moment, then a smile tugged at her lips. "I am a little interested in it myself."

Austin gave her an incredulous look. "And by interested, you mean..."

"I mean that perhaps it wouldn't be such a bad idea to learn how to defend myself. Perhaps I will need to use such skills one day."

"Those are choice words coming from the lady who is so determined to become a proper lady accepted by the ton."

"They don't have to know. I shan't go around announcing it at tea parties like you do."

This time the smile that cracked his expression lasted for more than a brief second. Austin looked at her as if he couldn't determine if she was joking or not, though his own eyes glittered with mirth.

"Very well then. Stand up."

Lavender lifted her brows in surprise. "Why?"

Austin stood and held out his hand to her. The gesture surprised her so much that Lavender simply froze. "I will teach you how to defend yourself," he told her.

She licked her lips, her throat suddenly dry. She didn't know why it took so much strength to take the hand he offered to her. And when she caught the shadow of a smile on his lips, her stomach started twisting in a manner that wasn't entirely uncomfortable. Lavender couldn't understand what this feeling was when she met his eyes. All she knew was that, at this moment, she didn't care about anything else.

***

"Hold your hands up, like this."

Lavender did as Austin told her to. He felt a tremor of amusement as she curled her hands into tiny fists and tried giving him the fiercest look she conjured. Which was akin to a kitten glaring up at a lion. Austin couldn't hold back the grin that took over his face.

"You look…" he began.

"Fearsome?" she replied. A smile tugged at her lips, even as she growled at him. "Terrifying? Am I making your knees tremble at the sight of me?"

Yes, but in a completely different manner.

Austin didn't dare say those words aloud. He didn't even know where that came from.

"You look as if you're in pain," he said instead and nearly laughed at the way her face fell. Even though something told him that it was bad idea, Austin stepped closer to her. The usual smell of lavender wrapped around him like a sweet embrace. He felt a jolt through his body as soon as he put his hand over hers to tighten her fist.

"Thumbs out," he ordered. "Keep them up. One arm closer to your side."

His demands were gruff and sharp but they didn't seem to bother her. In fact, Lavender appeared to be concentrating, clearly taking this far more seriously than he'd first thought.

"How do I look?" she asked once he took a step back.

Beautiful.

The word rushed to the tip of his tongue with such force that it took all his strength not to say anything. She caught his eye and he looked away, feeling heat crawling up his neck.

Austin cleared his throat. "Good enough," he answered. Then he went to stand before her. "Brace yourself."

Lavender's eyes widened. "Are you going to hit me?"

"No, you're going to hit me. And you will hurt your back if you do not open your legs a bit wider."

"Ah. I see." She did just that, then looked up at him expectantly.

The sight was like a punch to his gut. Something shifted in between them, an unnamed force so strong that Austin could do nothing but stare. He knew she was waiting for him to act but how could he come close to her now, when it felt as if his entire being was being pulled into her orbit and he would drown if he was not careful?

"Hit me," he managed to push out, his voice low and breathless. At her surprised look, he motioned to his midsection. "Right here. As hard as you can."

"But what if I hurt you?" she asked worriedly.

Austin would have laughed at that if it didn't feel as if his entire world was being tilted on its axis. "You won't," he assured instead.

He watched as she braced herself, as if gathering all the strength in her body to her fists. And then she struck. Austin could tell that she threw everything she could into the force of the blow and yet her fist glanced off his midsection like the brush of a feather.

"Oh, Dear God!" Lavender exclaimed, clutching her fist.

Austin was by her side in a second. "What is it? Are you hurt?"

She pressed her fist to her chest, eyes widening with tears. The sight stole his breath in the worst way possible. Austin didn't think twice about pulling her into his arms, guiding her back to the bench with one hand on the small of her back.

"Didn't that hurt you at all?" she whimpered softly to him, looking down at her fist. Austin could have sworn that it was throbbing.

He bit back a curse at himself. "I shouldn't have played along with this," he muttered. He took her hand in his and felt a surge of pressure in his temples when he saw how red her knuckles had become. "I should have known that you would have gotten hurt."

"And I should have known that punching you would have been no different than ramming my fist into a wall," she tried to joke, but it fell flat. "I can do better next time."

"There won't be a next time."

"Oh, nonsense," she said dismissively. "It will not hurt me to learn. Well...perhaps the first few times, but you've piqued my interest enough as it is. Now I know how best to form a fist if I ever find myself in danger."

"I won't let that happen," he found himself saying before he could stop himself. "You won't be in danger. Not while I am around."

"You cannot guarantee that. Will you follow me everywhere I go?"

"If I must." Silence followed his words. Austin focused on her hand, observing it for any signs of bruising or swelling. He didn't dare meet the eyes he knew were boring into him.

"I did not think you could be so honourable, my lord."

"Austin," he corrected gruffly. Against his better judgment, he looked up at her. Her brown eyes trapped him. "And you will be my wife. It will be my duty to protect you."

Lavender swallowed, searching his face as if looking for the truth in his words. There was no need to search very hard, she knew. It lay open and raw between them, so potent that it could not be ignored.

His eyes fell to her lips. She licked them at that moment. Austin didn't think she did it on purpose, didn't think she knew just how inviting they were. A voice in the back of his head told him to pull away even as he drew closer. Even as he heard her draw in a breath. Even as his heart ceased to beat and the only thing that could bring him back to life was her lips against his.

A clap of thunder boomed above them. Lavender yelped, leaping away from him. Austin didn't so much as flinch, even though his heart skipped a beat. Before either one of them could say anything, a sudden downpour showered them without warning.

"Come." Without waiting for her to respond, Austin seized her arm and pulled her in the direction of the house. Lavender, despite her far shorter legs, was able to keep up, clutching the skirt of her dress in one hand while she clung to his fingers with the other. The path was fast growing slick, their surroundings already hazy with the blur of the rain. Austin kept Lavender close to his side even as they delved under the cover of the back porch and into the house.

"Goodness, that came quite suddenly," Lavender gasped. "It is already storming!"

"You're shaking."

Lavender looked at him in surprise, as if she didn't notice the fact that her entire body shivered. Her hair was plastered to her neck and face, rivulets of water washing away the tears that had stained her cheeks previously. Austin ran his gaze down to her soaked dress, a lump suddenly forming in his throat.

Lavender followed his line of sight and gasped softly, taking a small step back. She wrapped her arms around herself.

Austin didn't move, looking anywhere but at her. "I shall have one of the maids fetch you a towel and dry clothes," he told her.

"Thank you, Austin."

Austin closed his eyes briefly, the sound of his name on her tongue washing over him. He didn't know what was happening. He understood male needs, had succumbed to it as often as any other healthy man in England. But this was something else, something that pulled desperate need from the depth of his soul. He just didn't quite know what that need was. All he knew was that the source of it stood before him, wet and quivering.

He lingered for a moment. For what, he didn't know. But he didn't want to leave just yet, even though the silence that stretched on quickly became uncomfortable. Only when Lavender began to hug her shoulders tighter did he break out of his daze long enough to remember what he should do.

"Follow me," he ordered before turning briskly away.

He listened to Lavender's water-sodden footsteps as they made their way upstairs to where the bedchambers were. She didn't say anything else. No mention of prizefighting, of teaching him how to be more gentlemanly. Nor of the kiss they had almost shared.

Austin came to a stop at the door of the bedchamber furthest from his own and turned to face her, clearing his throat. "It may not be as nice as what you are used to but—"

"I'm sure it will be just fine," Lavender said softly. She tried pushing her wet hair out of her face and failed. Austin curled his hand into fists.

He scratched the back of his head, unable to meet her eyes for some reason. "I shall see about the towels then."

He walked away before she could say anything in response. He didn't dare look back, didn't dare to think that she might be staring back at him.

Chapter Fifteen

True to his word, the towels and dry clothes came within minutes, while Lavender desperately tried to stave off the cold in front of the dying fire. To her disappointment, Austin did not show with them. The maids he'd sent hurried to help her, one rekindling the fire while the others dried her hair and helped her change. It only lasted a few minutes, which seemed like seconds considering her mind was far away from the room.

Her thoughts remained on that small bench in the garden, those heart-racing moments before the storm struck.

Every time she thought of how Austin had leaned closer to her, Lavender lost her breath. She'd frozen at the time but his gaze had rested solely on her lips so she doubted he had noticed. What would have happened if the thunder hadn't sounded? Would she have accepted the kiss?

Would he have kissed her?

Lavender brushed her fingers over her lips, a chill racing up her spine.

"Oh dear," one of the maids drying her hair said. "Miss, you are still cold. You are getting gooseflesh! Come, sit by the hearth."

She didn't wait for Lavender to respond before ushering her over to the armchair closest to the crackling fire. Lavender didn't bother to correct her. Gooseflesh washed her skin, yes, but it had nothing to do with her wet hair and everything to do with her soon-to-be husband somewhere in this house.

You will be my wife. It will be my duty to protect you.

A smile flitted over her face. Had he meant it or was he saying the things he thought he should as a respectable man?

"Where is the earl?" Lavender heard herself ask. She spoke so lowly that she didn't know if any of the maids heard her.

"He may be in his study, miss," one of them said.

Would it be too forward of her to go to see him? No, certainly not. He was her betrothed. She had no qualms with coming here, unchaperoned, before so why should it bother her now?

Only before there hadn't been a brief moment where she considered that he might like her more than she thought he did. Perhaps he was even beginning to fancy her...

An excited giggle escaped before she could do anything to stop it. Lavender stood and the maids fell away from her. She turned to face them. "Thank you for your assistance but—"

A knock on the door cut into her words. There was silence for a moment, and then a gruff, oddly hesitant voice. "Lavender?"

Lavender's heart shot into her throat. She ran her hands over hair, suddenly wishing it was a little drier. She knew she didn't look her best right now.

She cleared her throat, schooling her expression. "Yes?"

Another beat of silence and then, "May I come in?"

"Yes," she answered a little too quickly.

The door opened and Austin slid in, his eyes finding her immediately. His gaze started at her face, up to her hair, then slowly traveled down the length of her. Lavender felt exposed, heat washing through her body with such force that it chased away the lingering chill.

His eyes found hers again and then darted away as if he had just realized what he had been doing. The sight was both surprising and endearing

"Leave us," he ordered and the maids wasted no time scurrying out of the door, their heads bowed.

Lavender waited until they were alone. "They are afraid of you."

"As are many. I am no stranger to it."

"Do you like it?" she asked without thinking. "How intimidating you can be?"

For some reason, Austin stayed by the door. Almost as if he didn't dare to get any closer to her. "It matters not to me what others think of me. Though I will admit that my intimidating manner is at times favorable." He scratched the back of his head, still not looking at her. Instead, he seemed to be rather interested in the bed posts. "Do the clothes fit?"

"They are a bit loose." Lavender tugged on the slipping sleeve of the fine muslin gown she was wearing. "Was it the late countess'?'

"No, it was my mother's," Austin answered.

"Truly?' Lavender asked, her tone incredulous. She flushed, looking away. "Forgive me, I just—"

"It's fine. I understand your disbelief."

He hesitated again. It was so unusual to see that Lavender forgot the barrage of questions that had rushed to her head at the mention of the late countess and his mother.

"The evening is upon us," he went on as he wandered over to the closest window. "And this storm shows no signs of breaking soon."

"Yes, that appears to be the case," Lavender agreed. She drew nearer to the window as well. The skies were so dark and angry that it was almost as dark as nighttime. Wind and rain pounded the windowpanes with so much force that it was a wonder it didn't break right through.

"So I shall send word to your brother," Austin said. "He will worry when you do not return home."

"What will you tell him, Austin? That you have held me hostage at your house and have no intentions of returning me?"

He snorted, which she considered a success at her jest. "I shall tell him the truth. That you came to visit me late in the afternoon, without a chaperone, and that the current weather conditions make it impossible for you to return home."

"Oh, heavens, don't act as if you aren't happy to have me here." She came closer still, until she could peer up at his face. "Aren't you lonely here by yourself?"

"Not in the slightest." Austin glanced at her. Whatever he saw must have displeased him because he frowned a little and swallowed harshly. Without warning, he turned away, making his way to the door.

Lavender watched him go, feeling a little snubbed. She knew she was not the prettiest. Perhaps not even the smartest. But she had hoped that whomever she married would admire her individual charm. Did that mean that she was both unattractive *and* uninteresting?

Austin paused at the door, looking back at her. "You're going to be late if you intend on standing there all day."

Lavender perked up. "Pardon?"

"Dinner. It will be served shortly." Then he walked through the door.

She was left staring at the spot he'd just vacated, his last words ringing in her ears. There had to be something seriously wrong with her, she decided. Because why did that fill her with such giddiness?

Lavender hurried to the door and then paused to compose herself. She barrelled through right after, expecting to chase after him but she ran right into his chest instead.

"You will hurt yourself if you keep doing that," he commented dryly.

Lavender rubbed her nose, her grin peeking out from behind her hand. "I thought you had gone ahead of me."

"Perhaps I should have." He turned and began making his way down the hallway. Lavender noticed the fact that he was keeping pace with her. "But I do not want you to get lost on your way to the dining room. I'd hate to have to go in search of you."

"What an odd way of saying that you care about my well-being," Lavender chirped.

He scoffed. "I care more about a nosy lady poking her nose into rooms where she does not belong."

"Oh, so there are rooms that I have not seen yet. That is certainly good to know."

"Don't you dare think about it."

"Far too late for that, my lord," Lavender laughed. She nudged him playfully and he only grunted.

It only took them a couple of minutes to reach the dining room. Footmen stood at hand to serve the first course and Lavender did not miss the scowl Austin gave them.

"Are you uncomfortable?" she asked him.

He frowned at her. "No."

Lavender watched as he pulled her chair out for her and tried to swallow her surprise. "Yes, you are. The scowl on your face tells me that you are."

It only deepened. He took his seat and the footmen took that as their cue to move. "According to you, I am always scowling."

"Which is correct. And by now you should know that I am very rarely wrong. But it looks like a scowl of discomfort rather than your usual scowl of displeasure."

She didn't realize how crazy she sounded until he frowned at her as if she had two heads. Lavender avoided his eyes by watching the bowl of white soup being placed in front of her, along with all the cutlery and a glass of wine.

"You're right," he said after the footmen had retreated. "I am uncomfortable. I do not like being served my meals."

"Is this not what you are used to?"

"I prefer it being brought to my chambers or my study if I am unable to retrieve it myself. And I would do the latter more often if it were not for the kitchen help causing such a fuss every time I pay them a visit."

"Then why didn't you do the same this evening?" she asked, a beat before the answer to her question dawned on her. Lavender smiled. "If all this effort is for me, my lord, you needn't bother. I would have been quite fine with dining alone. I am used to it since Vincent is oftentimes away from home during dinnertime."

"It was not for you," he denied though there was something about the way he said it that made her doubt how truthfully he spoke. "I only thought that it would help if I got used to it from now, since I know you will be dragging me from dinner party to dinner party in the future."

"My goodness, Austin, I knew you would become more willing if I applied a bit more pressure on you. Yes, I do agree. This will certainly help you grow accustomed to such settings."

"God help me."

Lavender tilted her head to the side, regarding him with a soft smile. "Tell me about your childhood, Austin."

The sudden question seemed to startle him, though he covered it up quickly. "There is nothing to tell. It was like any other."

"I doubt that. You are the known bastard of England, pardon my bluntness. Surely that must have affected your upbringing in some manner."

Now he seemed to be paying keen attention to his soup, eating with the barest amount of grace as if he could not get through it quickly enough.

"As I've said, there is nothing to talk about. I'm sure yours is far more interesting than mine."

"Doubtful. To be quite honest with you, I was raised with a silver spoon in my mouth. Or perhaps I should say copper since it seems silver is only reserved for the upper class." Lavender paused, swallowing the note of bitterness that slipped out. Though she doubted Austin had missed it. "I wanted for nothing. I went to the best ladies' seminary in London and my studies consisted of everything that was to be expected of a daughter of a lord. Except my father was not a lord. He was a merchant. And it did not matter what we did, we were always treated as such."

"There is nothing wrong with being a merchant."

"Oh, I am well aware. And his success opened doors that others with titles could never open. But..." Lavender trailed off. Rage and bitterness turned her stomach, making her wish she didn't have to continue eating. It took every bit of her strength to suppress those familiar feelings, not needing Austin to see any of it.

He wouldn't understand. Even Vincent didn't understand, even though he went along with it to appease her. And she didn't expect them to. They weren't there when she saw her father return home late at night, heavily inebriated and furious. They hadn't secretly followed him to his study and watched as he drunk himself into a stupor. They didn't see shades of who he had once been fade away until he was nothing but a shell of his former self. Vincent thought it foolish, that their father had given up on life and on them. But Lavender understood the depth of her father's pain—and the root of it.

She'd spent years trying to hide the anger that simmered deep within her. It was never far away, always within reach. She could call on it when she needed motivation to continue on her path and it never steered her wrong. But she knew better than to let anyone see the dark, roiling knot that existed deep within her.

For a few moments, Austin stared at her as if he could see that ball she'd tucked away. She was afraid of the question that he would ask next, not completely certain that she'd be able to deflect it like she usually did.

But instead he said, "Well, since you had all those lessons, I suppose I could ask for a worse instructor to teach me how to be a proper gentleman."

Lavender looked at him in surprise. He knew something. Perhaps not the truth but that there was more to what she was saying. And instead of pressing her on it, he decided to change the topic.

She smiled in relief. "I hope to be thanked in the future for the kind service I am extending to you," she said, to which he only grunted.

There was no more talk about the past after that. The dinner went by in relative comfort and, to Lavender's surprise, Austin was far more talkative than he let on. She even got him to laugh a few times throughout the three courses that were served and by the time they were finished with dessert, he seemed content, swirling his glass of wine idly.

"It does not seem as if the storm is letting up," he commented.

Lavender paused. Even in the dining room, she could hear the thunder of rain outside, a low drone that she had been ignoring this entire time. The thought of not being able to go home should have bothered her. Instead she felt immense relief.

"It is not," she agreed. "It appears as if I will be spending the night."

Austin raised his brows at her. "You sound oddly pleased by that."

"Do I?"

The barest of smiles touched his face. "Then I suppose I should keep you entertained while you are here. You like to read, correct?"

"It is one of my favourite pastimes." Lavender paused then shook her head. "My only pastime."

"Then come with me and I shall show you my library." He stood and held out his hand. Butterflies fluttered in the pit of her stomach as she took it and came to a stand.

They left the dining room behind. And though he released her hand after a few seconds, Lavender realized at that moment that she was willing to follow him anywhere.

Chapter Sixteen

The library looked better than the last time she'd seen it. It had been in passing, when Austin had been showing her around the house and informing her of the renovations that would be done in each room. When she'd come here last, the bookshelves had been stripped of all their books, looking bare and lifeless.

Now the shelving was restored, broken joints and chipped surfaces made anew. And every nook and cranny of the bookshelves was cramped with books, making Lavender gasp in awe the moment she entered. It might be the largest room in the house, she realized, with enough armchairs and chaise lounges for there to be a comfortable literary session with a few of her closest friends. There was even a writing desk tucked in the corner. At the sight of it, she immediately thought of herself writing letters or journal entries on a beautiful sunny morning.

"Do you like it?"

If she hadn't known better, she would have thought that Austin sounded hesitant just now. Almost as if he truly cared about what she thought about the room.

Lavender looked back at him. He was leaning against the door jamb, hands tucked into his pockets. "It was the late countess' favourite room in the house. She loved reading but in her last few years alive, she did not get the chance to return to London. The room fell into disrepair, like so many other rooms in the house."

"I think it's utterly beautiful, Austin," Lavender said honestly. She made her way to the closest bookshelf and gasped when she realized that nearly every edition of Shakespeare's work was tucked within. "She must have been quite the collector."

"She was. Father spared no expense when it came to her hobbies. I suppose that was one of his ways of apologising."

He didn't have to clarify. Lavender turned to face him. "This is quite lovely, Austin. It truly is. But I think there is something else I would rather do than read this evening. And I would love it if you could join me."

"What is that?" he asked with a frown.

Lavender grinned. "Do you have any more wine?"

Austin raised his brow in question but she could see his own playful smile tugging at his lips. "I have something far better than wine. If you think you can handle it."

Lavender sank onto the closest chaise lounge, watching as he crossed over the room to the sideboard. "If it is whiskey or brandy you speak of, then it does not frighten me. I was quite the rebellious child, you see. And I would sneak into my father's sideboard many times to try a few."

"A few?" he echoed, incredulous. "I'm surprised you were not turned away from it after the first sip."

"Oh, I was tempted to," Lavender laughed. "But there was something about that heartrending burn that drew me back time and time again."

Austin poured two glasses of what Lavender assumed was scotch as he chuckled. The sound greatly startled her, causing her heart to palpitate. It was the first time she'd ever heard it in actual mirth, the sound deep enough to resonate throughout her entire being.

If Austin noticed her slight change in demeanor, he did not show it. He brought the drink over to her, and handed her the scotch with a raised brow. "I shall believe it when I see it," he said in a challenging tone. And perhaps there was even a hint of teasing in there as well.

Lavender's smile faltered momentarily as she experienced a pleasant warmth spreading throughout her chest. "Challenge accepted, my lord."

She didn't know what possessed her to do what she did next. It certainly had something to do with Austin's proximity to her and the fading echoes of his laughter ringing in her ears. It might even have something to do with the way she felt, as if he had set her on fire and held the snuffer in his hands. Lavender didn't question her next actions though questioning herself and everything around her was all she usually did.

She tipped the glass at her lips and downed it all in one go.

"Are you mad, woman?" Austin shouted, snatching the glass from her hand.

But it was too late. The burning liquid was already tearing through her throat, steadily making its way down her gullet and to her stomach. Lavender felt tears spring to her eyes even as she grinned victoriously. "Do you believe me now?"

"I believe that you might have lost your mind."

She couldn't hold it in any longer. Coughs richocheted up her throat with such force that she doubled over. She was only vaguely aware of Austin holding her by her arms and patting her back. It took everything in her to keep from sinking to her knees.

"Blast it, woman, there wasn't any reason to do that." Lavender couldn't tell if she heard annoyance or amusement in his voice. Perhaps a mixture of both.

"I know," Lavender wheezed. Somehow, she found a chair. Austin kept hovering over her—rubbing and patting her back, brushing her hair from her face. "Honestly, I don't know what possessed me to do such a thing either. Your bad influence, maybe?"

"My bad influence?" Now it was definitely amusement. "I cannot believe you. How are you feeling now?"

"Better," she confessed. She wiped the tears from her cheeks, blinking them away from her vision. "I thought I saw the light for a moment, but it has passed."

Austin chuckled again. The sound was comforting. "Perhaps you should not drink anything else for the rest of the evening then."

"Yes, I think that would be a good idea." She managed a smile. "I hope you will not find me too unladylike if I opt to sit on the floor?"

Lavender didn't bother to wait for his response before sliding out of the armchair and sinking to the cool, wooden floor. It helped to ground her since her head was already beginning to spin. Downing such strong alcohol after sipping on wine at dinner was not a wise choice.

To her surprise, Austin hunkered down next to her. All of a sudden, Lavender remembered her state. She touched her hair and was horrified to find that it was quickly drying into knots. Not to mention the tear she had just shed would quickly turn her cheeks into splotchy messes. And the sleeve of her dress would not stay up, for goodness sake.

She tugged it up, avoiding Austin's eyes and the silence that settled over them.

"Perhaps I should have them find a dress that fits you better," he mused after a moment.

"There's no need," she said quickly, her words slurring together. "This is quite fine. Quite a beautiful dress, I must say, which surprises me considering who it had belonged to."

She froze, heart stilling. Why did she just say that? Had the scotch gone straight to her head rather than her stomach?

Lavender didn't dare to look at Austin, afraid to see just how badly she had ruined the comfortable atmosphere that had settled between them.

"You're right," he said after a moment. "A mere maid possessing a gown as nice as that one is not often seen among our people. My father was simply a giving man. And he loved my mother in a way that he could never give the countess."

Lavender didn't know what to say at first. That was the most he had ever spoken about his father's infidelity. She was on cracking ice, she realized. If she was careful, she might be able to make it to the other end where the full truth lay.

"What was she like?" she asked after a moment. "Your mother."

He sat cross-legged, his back resting on the armchair. His eyes strayed to the unlit hearth instead of her, which was just fine. It gave her all the time she needed to look at him. Watching the shadows play over his face, the depth of his eyes as he fell into the past, the tick of his sharp jaw. Goodness, she'd always known that he was handsome but watching him now stole her breath away.

"She was…no one. And everything." Austin's voice was softer than she'd ever heard it, forcing her to lean in to listen. "She was only a maid and to men like my father, that should have meant nothing. But my father was not like other lords. Or perhaps my mother was not like most maids. For the most part, she stayed in her place, kept her head down, and remained out of sight. But when she was with my father, she was truly happy—despite what became of her after I was born."

"What happened?" Lavender breathed.

"I do not know the details, I'm afraid. In my youth, I did not want to know anything about their affair because I was ashamed of it. I was ashamed of who I was because of it and I hated the way I was treated. Never a part of any world, a complete outcast."

He laughed humorlessly. "Doesn't it sound odd hearing such a thing from me? Perhaps that is why I am the way that I am now."

"You are perfect the way that you are," Lavender said without thought. His eyes darted to her and she quickly looked away, cheeks flaring with heat. "But it sounds as if your parents were truly in love."

"As much as a lord and maid could be, but they were doomed to fail, of course."

"Because of the late countess?'

"Among other societal pressures." He sipped his drink. Lavender noticed it seemed a little more difficult for him to swallow this time.

"Did she ever..."

"Resent me?" Something passed over his face, warm and comforting. "No, she accepted me as one of her own, even though she could not forgive my father for what he had done. I have nothing but love and respect for her. For my parents as well, in their own way."

Lavender shifted closer. "I must admit that it is quite a relief to know that you were treated kindly. So many others would not be able to say the same."

Austin frowned at her, confused. "Why should you feel any relief at all?"

"Because you were accepted, despite it all. And while your peers might have treated you like an outcast, at least you did not have to suffer through the same thing in the comfort of your own home."

He simply stared at her for a moment before he said, "I did not think about it that way."

Lavender smiled and hoped it would distract him from the fact that she was inching closer still. "There is one more thing I wish to tell you, Austin."

His nostrils flared. Despite that, he kept himself completely still. "What is that?"

"I am not afraid of you."

Lavender did not know what came over her. Perhaps it was the darkness that washed the room or the raging storm outdoors. It could have been the cool flooring beneath them, the roar of alcohol in her veins, or perhaps the raw truth that had spilled from Austin's lips. It could even be the way he looked at her right now, like she was a mythical beauty that he could hardly believe was real.

Whatever it was, Lavender latched onto it. She let it drive her actions until she was so close that she could feel his breath against her cheek. She raised a hand to his cheek, brushing a thumb across the rough stubble that was already starting to sprout.

"I see you," she murmured. "The way you wish to be seen."

Austin searched her face. For a moment, Lavender felt a bite of fear, realizing how wildly inappropriate she was being at the moment. She was an unchaperoned, unmarried woman in a man's home. If others were to find out about this, they would not care that said man was her intended. The scandal that could come out of this...she didn't want to think about it. She wouldn't. The only person she cared about right now was sitting before her.

"Lav..."

She felt so many things in this moment. Fear, uncertainty, longing, want. Above all, she felt something fearsome crashing into her at the whisper of her name, capable of tearing her into small bits at the slightest touch. Lavender knew what it meant at that moment, even though she didn't dare to think the words. She only needed to exist in this moment. This beautiful, all-consuming moment.

She opened her mouth, hoping the right words would pour out. "Austin, I—"

His lips came crashing down on hers. Lavender's heart hitched in her throat then ceased to beat altogether. His arm snaked around her waist, tugging her into his chest. Just like everything else in his life, he took what he wanted and Lavender was more than happy to comply.

But the kiss was gentler than she expected, tender. Though he held her as if he didn't want to ever let her go, he kissed her as if she were precious and fragile, soft touches and a loving swipe of the tongue. Lavender thought she might have moaned against his lips. Maybe that was him? Either way, she didn't want this moment to ever end.

Her prayers fell on deaf ears. All too soon, he pulled away, but stayed close enough. "We shouldn't do this," he murmured.

Lavender couldn't help her smile of amusement. "I did not think you to be the type who cares about society's etiquette."

"I don't." His voice was rougher than she'd ever heard it, his attention moving from her lips to her eyes then back to her lips. "But I know that you do."

That touched her in ways that she could hardly manage. That feeling came rushing back again, overwhelming her to such a degree that she was forced to pull away before she said or did something foolish.

"You're right," she murmured, getting to her feet. Austin rose as well, not taking his eyes off her for a second. Being under such close scrutiny made her feel too aware of herself. Her disheveled, half-dried hair. Her slightly too big nightgown. Yet the look in his eyes...

"Come." Austin took her hand without warning. Lavender smiled as he began leading her out of the library. They said nothing, their fingers entwined. There was nothing left to be said. They'd stepped into a new territory where he was no longer the uncouth, unwilling lord and she was no longer the excitable, plotting sister of a merchant. They were just man and woman, soon to be husband and wife. They were so much more than what she had needed initially.

A sense of peace settled over her as he led her back to the bedchamber she had changed in. He brought her as far as the bed and, for a moment, Lavender was almost certain—and excited—that he would crawl into the bed right next to her. But instead, he released her hand and took a small step back.

Lavender hid her slight disappointment as she got under the covers. The moment she did, he surprised her by leaning down to press a kiss on her forehead. Goodness, it was as if he wanted her to melt right into this bed.

"Goodnight, Lav," he murmured softly.

"Goodnight, Austin," she whispered.

The absence of his touch nearly had her calling him back. But Lavender said nothing as she watched him retreat to the door. Austin looked back only once, neither smiling nor scowling. But there was something on his face that sparked hope and happiness in the depths of her heart.

Then he was gone and Lavender was left alone, knowing all too well that there would be no hope of sleep tonight.

Chapter Seventeen

Austin didn't sleep at all last night. Honestly, after everything that had happened, he was a little grateful that he couldn't. A part of him was a little afraid to acknowledge the possibility of the enchanting pair of brown eyes following him into his dreams.

But she trailed his thoughts constantly, hounding him. He went from attempting to sleep to pacing his bedchamber to resigning himself to his study instead. No matter what he did, he could not get her out of his head. He could still feel the phantom touch of Lavender's lips against his.

Dawn came far too slowly. Austin was exhausted by then, his lack of sleep the night before catching up to him. Even so, he felt oddly invigorated knowing that, in a matter of hours, Lavender would be up again.

He waited. He paced. He walked through the garden, distracting himself by admiring how everything looked put together despite the storm that had raged the night before. Now there was nothing but blue skies and a blazing sun, as if nothing had happened at all. When he thought the time was appropriate, he got Mr. Francis to have breakfast ready in the drawing room. Then he sat there, staring up at the portrait of the late countess wondering how his life had turned to this.

"My, you're up early."

Austin turned slowly, calmly, even though his heart skipped a beat and it felt as if every raging thought in his mind had quieted to nothing.

Lavender stood at the threshold of the drawing room, a small smile on her lips. She wore something different, a pale blue morning gown that he believed had once belonged to the late countess. It fit her far better than his late mother's had. Austin swallowed, steeling his nerves and resisting the urge to take in every inch of her appearance before finally settling on her face.

She'd brushed her hair but didn't bother to style it. He had to admit that he liked it that way, though she would look just as lovely with her hair done up in ringlets like the other ladies of the ton. Watching her pad up to him with bare feet and her hair tumbling untethered down her back did something to him that he could not comprehend.

He cleared his throat and looked away. "Did you sleep well?"

"Not very," she admitted, sitting in the chair across from him. "My mind was a little...preoccupied."

"Was it?" Why couldn't he meet her eyes? Austin had never cared to pay pieces of toast and jam so much attention before now.

"How about you? You look as if you haven't slept at all."

She said her words in jest but when he glanced up at her, her brows raised in surprise.

"Didn't you?"

"I suppose my mind was a little preoccupied as well."

Lavender just stared at him for a moment. And then her smile widened knowingly. She began pouring herself a cup of green tea. "Well, I hope you are not too tired, Austin, since there are still a lot of preparations we need to undergo for this Season. Like the tailor's visit tomorrow afternoon. And—"

"Pray tell, don't you think about anything other than your silly little plan?"

Her brows dipped. "It isn't a silly little plan. I have been devising this for as long as I can remember and I only have a limited amount of time to execute it."

"All for the aim of impressing a lady who has no respect for you nor your family."

He struck a nerve. Austin realized it a moment after he said his words and instantly regretted it. This wasn't how he'd intended for their morning to go. He thought they could talk comfortably over breakfast then perhaps go for one of those walks she was so fond of before returning to her home. But as he watched her smile slip into a scowl, Austin realized that he'd just ruined their chances of that.

"Impressing? Surely after everything you do not still think that I only wish to impress the countess?"

Since he'd already gotten this deep, he couldn't help but say, "What else could it possibly be?"

She drew in a slow breath as if she was trying to calm herself. "Austin, I think you of all people would understand how degrading it is to be around those who deem you as inferior."

"I do," he admitted. "Which is why I cannot understand why you want to be accepted by such people."

"Because it was my father's only wish to be." Austin leaned back, watching as she slowly sipped her tea. "My father grew up in poverty and created a name and wealth for himself. He gave my brother and I a comfortable life. Even after my mother passed away, when I was only seven, he did all he could to raise us. I always respected him for that, loved him dearly for everything he'd done for us."

Lavender drew in a breath. Austin could almost see the layers of her composure peeling away from her skin as she spoke. With every breath, raw emotion began to shine through to the surface. Right now, he saw nothing but such deep sadness that he wished he could go back in time and take back the words that had caused it.

"He wanted more for us. We were always stuck in between, you see. Wealthy enough to be deemed a part of the upper class, but lacking the prestige and honour that came with a title. He thought that if he could get us accepted by them then our lives would be infinitely better." She laughed but it lacked its usual humor. "Those were excuses, of course. My father idolized the idea of becoming a lord and thought that he could be granted land and a title if he befriended the right people. He tried so hard that when they eventually rejected and humiliated him in front of the ton, it sent him into deep melancholy. I was young at the time, too young to understand just how embarrassing it had been. Apparently, it was enough of a scandal to fill the scandal sheets for weeks on end. He became the laughingstock of the ton."

She sipped her tea again and another layer peeled away. Under the sadness, Austin saw anger and resentment blazing in her eyes. "My father, the proud man that he was, could not handle it. He drank himself to sleep every night after that. He turned away from us. He was a shell of his former self. When he finally passed away, a part of me thought that it was a mercy, that perhaps now he was a bit happier. Before he died, though, I made him promise to use his connections to find me a husband. I needed one, you see. Not for love or to start a family but because I was well aware of how crucial having a husband would be to executing my plan."

"Your plan of revenge," Austin said as realization dawned on him.

Lavender met his eyes. She held her composure well enough but there was no concealing the rage that shimmered there.

"The Countess of Lively pulls the strings of the ton. She was the one who degraded my father until he felt like a failure, despite everything he had built for us. You've seen firsthand how scathing her words can be, even as she says them with a smile. I intend to show her that sitting on such a high throne will only make her fall that much more painful."

After that, nothing else was said. Lavender blinked and the mask—the mask he hadn't even realized until now that she'd had in place from the moment he met her—was back in place. She resumed eating as if nothing were amiss, as if she hadn't just revealed to him that she had been consumed with vengeance all these years.

He didn't know the right words to say and it bothered him. He should apologize at least, for misunderstanding her, but before he could get the words out, the door banged open.

Vincent Latrice came marching in, face red with anger. "Lavender!" he barked, making his sister jump.

"Vincent?" Lavender sounded confused. "What are you doing here?"

"Why do you think I am here, my foolish, insane sister?" He stalked towards her, dragging his fingers through his hair. "Do you know how worried I was about you all night?"

"But Austin sent word—"

"Which did not reach me until this morning! Do you think anyone in their right mind would have braved last night's storm to deliver a simple message?" Vincent whirled on Austin. "And you! Surely you should have known better than to house an unmarried lady without a chaperone overnight?"

Austin raised a brow at him as he asked, "What would you have had me do? Send her home in the storm?"

"Vincent, please," Lavender stepped in before Vincent could think of a response. She stood, putting a placating hand on her brother's arm. "It was my fault. I was the one who decided to come here without warning and Austin only did what he thought was best at the moment."

He pulled his fingers through his hair again, frustrated. It was a wonder how he didn't pull a few strands loose at the same time, Austin thought.

"You're going to be the death of me, Lav," he sighed. "Come. It's time to go home."

Lavender pouted. "Can't I stay and finish break—" At Vincent's scathing look, she quickly said, "Or not. Let's leave."

"I'll walk you to the door," Austin said, standing. He met Vincent's eyes, challenging him to say something about it.

The other man only shook his head in frustration. They left the drawing room in silence, making their way to the foyer. Austin could see Mr. Francis hovering anxiously nearby, holding a pair of slippers in his hand.

At the door, Lavender turned to Austin. "Thank you for hosting me, my lord. I hope to repay your kindness one day."

Austin resisted the urge to grin at that. How proper of her to say, considering the fact that she was still bare-footed. As if she was just now realizing that herself, she accepted her now dried slippers from Mr. Francis.

"Yes, thank you," Vincent joined in, looking considerably less frustrated now. "And forgive my anger, my lord. I was just worried sick about her all night that I rushed over here as soon as I received your letter. I understand that my rash sister is the one at fault here."

"Or perhaps no one is at fault," Lavender suggested lightheartedly. When she caught her brother's glare, she thinned her lips. "You're not in the mood for jests, I see. Austin, we should leave before my brother's glaring gives him a megrim."

Austin swallowed his laughter and nodded. "Very well."

He stepped back, his throat suddenly growing thick as he watched Lavender and her brother leave. He followed them to the porch and listened to their soft bickering as they climbed into their waiting carriage. He didn't move until their carriage was out of sight.

At last, he turned and went back into the house, ignoring Mr. Francis still hovering in the corner. He hated to admit it to himself but the truth was as bright as day.

Now that Lavender was gone, the house seemed much, much lonelier.

***

The first thing Lavender noticed when she reached home was that there were two other carriages in the driveway. She frowned at Vincent. "Do you have guests over?"

Vincent didn't look at her. Lavender had almost forgotten just how much her brother could hold a grudge. It may be days before he forgave her for this.

"You worried more people than you think," he grumbled as the carriage came to a stop.

She didn't bother to question him further on it. Later she would try to get him to forgive her, hoping she could simply lay on the charm like she usually did. She wasn't often denied anything and her brother's forgiveness was normally one of it. But this was her first time doing something as scandalous as this so she wasn't sure just how easy it would be this time around.

Lavender put it to the back of her mind as she exited the carriage and made her way into the house. The moment she stepped past the threshold, someone barrelled up to her.

"Lavender! Are you all right? Are you hurt? Did that brute hurt you?"

A pair of hands gripped her shoulders and began twisting her around. Lavender just barely caught the familiar head of blond hair and worried blue eyes. "Colin, what are you doing here?"

He kept twisting her around as if he was checking for wounds or bruises. Lavender glimpsed Alice over his shoulder, looking at them with a mixture of relief and humor. "Alice? Goodness, you're here as well?"

"How could I not be?" Alice said. "Vincent came to my home early this morning asking if you might have been here. When I told him that I haven't seen you since the tea party, he informed me that you didn't come home last night. Considering the storm last night, I grew worried and followed him here."

Lavender pushed Colin's hands away before he made her dizzy. "And you?" she asked. "Did he come to you too?"

"He was here before," Vincent grumbled from behind. "I hope you see the extent to which your actions have consequences, Lav."

"Yes, yes, I understand." She took a step back to face them all. "I'm sorry, everyone, for the way I worried you. I assure you, though, that I was in good hands."

Colin snorted. "Good hands? You were at the Earl of Derby's house."

Lavender frowned at him. She couldn't understand the anger in his voice. Colin had never been angry with her before and now it had happened twice. "Yes, but I was perfectly safe, as you can see. And as soon as the stormed cleared, Austin sent word of where I was to Vincent."

"Austin?" Colin looked two shades paler. "Have you two grown so close?"

Lavender didn't get the chance to think of a response to that before Alice came up to her side, sliding her arm through hers. "If she says that she was safe, then I believe her. There isn't any need to hound her now. Let us just be happy that she is here."

Vincent sighed dramatically. "I suppose I should sent a letter of apology to Lord Derby. I was rather rude when I arrived."

"I'm happy you realised it," Lavender said. "Though I doubt he really took your words to heart."

Colin paced away, looking agitated. He moved over to the staircase and leaned against the balustrade with his arms crossed, a scowl on his face. Lavender frowned at him. She couldn't understand why he seemed so...frustrated.

But she didn't want to ask him about it right now. She was tired, since she hadn't slept much last night, and felt a little overwhelmed at the high emotions circling the room at the moment. She could get answers about why Colin was here before Vincent had gone to see Alice or when Vincent would stop sulking about it.

"If you all do not mind," she began, making her way to the staircase. "I am quite tired and wish to retire to my chambers."

"I shall come with you," Alice announced, not letting go of Lavender's arm. The look in her eye told Lavender that there was a reason for it so she didn't bother to protest.

"Very well then." Vincent began heading in the direction of the hallway next to the staircase. "Mr. Asher, let us finish our discussion, shall we?"

Discussion? Lavender paused, watching as the scowling Colin avoided her eyes and followed behind her brother. What could they possibly be discussing?

Probably business matters, she dismissed after a moment. She didn't care about such things.

Suddenly too tired to question anything, Lavender made her way up to her chambers with Alice by her side. The moment she was in her bedchamber, she collapsed onto the bed with her arms and legs spread wide, watching as Alice absently made her way to the sofa next to the fire place.

Exhaustion settled over her eyes the moment she sank into her bed. But Lavender knew she couldn't sleep just yet. She knew Alice well enough to know that there was a reason she had followed her up here.

True to what she'd expected, Alice sat with her hands clasped in her lap, staring expectantly at Lavender.

"Out with it," Lavender sighed. "I know you have your questions."

"Quite a few," Alice admitted with a private smile. "But before that, I do hope you understand how worried you made everyone."

"I did not think word would reach to both Colin and you," Lavender sighed. "But yes, I suppose I should have been more mindful. Though, I must add that there wasn't anything I could do at the time."

"Yes, I am aware. Which is why I am opting to hold back most of my chastisement. Now, for the questions." Alice leaned forward and rested her chin on her lap, her elbow balancing on her knee. "How was it spending the night with the Earl of Derby?"

Lavender turned her face away to hide the blush that suddenly rushed to her cheeks. Slowly, she sat up and ran her fingers idly through her hair, giving herself enough time to think of the right answer.

What was the right answer? She'd done so many scandalous things in the past few hours that she was afraid of saying it aloud. She knew that her secret was safe with Alice but saying it would be admitting aloud things she was yet to admit to herself just yet.

So she settled on skirting around the full truth as best as she could. "He was a gracious host," she said and then cringed inwardly when she heard how unbelieving that was. "Well, as gracious a host as the earl could be. You know his temperament as well as I do."

"Perhaps not as well as you do," Alice hummed, that smile still playing around her lips. Almost as if she knew more than she was letting on. "What possessed you to go there unchaperoned in the first place?"

"I am not sure," Lavender admitted. "I had time on my hands and thought that it would be a good idea to prepare him for what was to come. Things took quite a turn, however."

"In what way?"

"Well...there was the storm."

"And?"

Lavender frowned at her. Did she know about the kiss? Surely she didn't? Or was she simply reading the blush on Lavender's face and assuming that something might have happened?

"And...nothing," Lavender said finally, avoiding her eyes.

Alice laughed. "You are a magnificent liar, Lavender, but you have never been able to lie to me. Something happened. I noticed it the moment you walked through the door. And I think Colin might be thinking the same thing."

"Nothing happened and Colin was only worried about me, like you said." Lavender felt a bite of guilt at the lie. Alice said nothing and the silence bore down on her until she couldn't help but crack. "All right, perhaps something did happen."

"I knew it!" In a second, Alice flew across the room onto the bed. "Tell me all about it."

"It really isn't anything!" Lavender quickly said. "We only shared a few intimate conversations. It gave me a chance to understand who he truly was. And..."

"And..."

Lavender's lips tilted up as the memory of their lips touching filled her mind. There was no chance of her hiding it at this point. "We may have shared a kiss."

Alice, being nearly as dramatic as Lavender was behind closed doors, squealed. Lavender tried putting her hand over Alice's mouth but it wasn't enough to hold back the sound.

"Hush!" Lavender scolded. "Vincent and Colin might hear you!"

"Oh, yes." Alice sobered up quickly, though her eyes danced with excitement. "We wouldn't want that, would we? Tell me how it happened, when, everything."

Her excitement was infections. Honestly, even though she had spent the better part of last night thinking about their kiss, Lavender hadn't truly come to terms with it. The man she had sat with this morning had been the same standoffish man she'd met, making her wonder if he cared about the kiss as much as she did.

But Alice's excitement had the same feeling bubbling up in her and, before she knew it, Lavender was telling her every detail about her time with Austin from the moment she walked into his study until the second he kissed her goodnight.

It felt nice, she realized after a while, to simply sit and talk with her friends about mundane things such as kissing and feelings. She could admit to Alice that she might be falling for Austin. It didn't seem so terrifying to say it aloud to her friend. It didn't feel as if she was jumping headfirst into something that would leave her a broken mess in the end. Instead, she chatted and laughed and squealed about everything that had happened as if this wasn't an arranged marriage. As if she wasn't dragging an unwilling man around to help her in a quest for revenge.

As if she hadn't known about her brother's plan to 'trap' her future husband in a contract by paying him off to marry her and that that was the only reason why Austin tolerated her presence.

With Alice, Lavender could almost pretend as if Austin might be falling in love with her too.

Chapter Eighteen

Lavender was rather pleased with herself and had been since her walk through Hyde Park. How could she not be after she'd convinced one of the most difficult of men she'd ever met into attending the tailor with her and her brother? It was like wrangling a raging bull into a pen.

So pleased was she that she had not been able to wipe that smile off her face all throughout breakfast. Thankfully her brother had an early morning meeting to attend to and was not around to question her on why she was in such a good mood. What would she have said?

I am excited to purchase new clothing for Lord Derby so that he will look more like a proper earl while we carry out my plan for revenge?

It sounded odd even to her. But she couldn't help the mounting excitement as soon as she was done with breakfast and headed up to her chambers to fetch her reticule and her bonnet. She told herself that she had many lovely dresses and she hadn't put on this beautiful blue morning gown because she knew she would be seeing Austin today.

By the time she made it back downstairs, she saw Vincent in the foyer, returning home from his meeting.

"Vincent," she greeted happily. "I hope you are not too tired because it will soon be time for us to leave for the tailor's. Lord Derby will be arriving at any moment."

"While we wait for him, why don't we have a talk in the parlour?" Vincent suggested in a serious tone. He didn't wait for her to respond, heading to the parlor instead.

Lavender frowned at the back of his head but said nothing as she trailed after him. She kept her question at bay until they were safely behind closed doors. Then she asked, "What is the matter, Vincent? Did something bad happen?"

"No, no nothing of the sort," he assured her.

She ventured over to an armchair and sat, still frowning. "What do you want to talk about then?"

"You, Lav," he said. He chose the chair directly across from her, looking concerned. "Do you truly want to be betrothed to the Earl of Derby?"

"Why are you asking me this all of a sudden?"

"Because I understand that I might have sprung this decision on you a little too quickly, without giving you much say in the matter. I have never been the type to control your life, Lav, so if this is not what you truly want then you should tell me."

"You know I want to be married. I was the one who pressured you into enforcing Father's old promise in the first place."

"You did," Vincent agreed. "But I chose the man for you. I did not even think that perhaps there might be other options. Like a love match, for example."

"A love match?" she echoed. "Pardon me but I am quite confused by all of this. Where is this coming from?"

Vincent propped one leg over the other. "You should know that another gentleman has asked me for your hand in marriage. And this gentleman claims to be truly in love with you."

"Surely you jest!"

Vincent chuckled, clearly taken aback by her surprise. Lavender couldn't even smile back. She watched as her brother nodded. "I was quite shocked as well. And then I began to wonder if perhaps it would have been better if you married someone who actually loved you, even if you do not feel the same way about them."

"Who is it?" she asked. "Who told you that they loved me?"

"I would rather not say. Only because he swore me to secrecy."

"But I am your sister!"

"And because I know you, I want you to truly think about whether you want to be betrothed to the earl before I tell you who it is, lest it cloud your judgment."

"My judgment won't be clouded, I assure you. Tell me who it is."

Vincent laughed again. "I should have known better than to think you would let this go easily. Promise me you will think about what I am saying, Lav?"

Lavender let out a frustrated breath. If Vincent was determined to do something, there was no changing his mind. She supposed that was another thing they had in common. "Very well. I shall think about it."

"Good."

"But I must say," she went on. "That it isn't as if I have not already given my situation some thought. And, after spending some time with Lord Derby, I've come to realise that he is not as bad as I first thought. Perhaps what we have is not love but I believe we have something akin to friendship. With time, he just may show me the sort of man he is deep inside."

"Hm." Vincent took that all in with a simple nod. "Let us hope whatever decision you decide to make is for the best. Again, you are in control here."

"Thank you, Vincent." Lavender stood and made her way over to him, bending to plant a kiss on his cheek. Just as she straightened, Henry appeared to announce the arrival of the Earl of Derby. She thanked God Vincent was not looking when a bright smile stretched across her face in response.

She managed to tuck that smile away as they both went out to greet Austin. The moment she laid eyes on him, her steps faltered. He'd shaven and styled his hair again. How could this man get any more handsome? Not to mention the fact that the bruises were nearly all gone.

"My lord," Vincent greeted, sticking out a hand to Austin. "It is good to see you again."

"Likewise," Austin muttered, accepting the hand. Lavender's heart skipped a beat when he looked at her. "Lavender."

"Austin," she said, her voice softer than she'd like. It was hard breathing when he looked at her so directly. Did he notice the dress? She hoped he did.

"Shall we?" Vincent asked, cutting in the moment. He gestured for Austin to take the lead. Austin did just that, giving Lavender the chance to get her breathing under control.

She trailed behind the two men as they made their way to the carriage. Vincent attempted to engage Austin in conversation about the weather—a shoddy attempt, she thought—and then gave up after Austin's third unintelligible grunt. Lavender hid her amusement as she climbed into the carriage behind them and they set off for the tailor.

Austin wasn't happy about this. He didn't have to say as much because his face told it all. His usual displeased demeanor seemed more sour than usual and it was a wonder he wasn't complaining the entire way there. Instead, silence filled the carriage as they made their way to Bond Street. Despite the discomfort in the air, Lavender was at peace. A part of her hadn't expected to make it this far.

"I told the tailor that we would be coming," she informed Austin when they arrived. "So we should have the shop to ourselves."

"Wonderful," he drawled sarcastically. "I was worried about that."

Lavender rolled her eyes. "I knew you would be."

He did the same then shook his head as he made for the door. Vincent lingered behind, staring after him.

"Don't worry, Vincent," Lavender told him, patting him on the shoulder. "Austin simply doesn't like mornings."

"I have a feeling he isn't happy at any time of the day," Vincent said under his breath. "Are you certain about this, Lav?"

She didn't respond, not entirely sure how to. Her excitement earlier was beginning to falter in the face of Austin's obvious reluctance to be here. They'd had such a nice time for the past couple of days that she'd forgotten just how cantakerous he was. What if this was a mistake?

She didn't say any of that, gesturing to her brother to go inside the tailor's shop instead. Mr. Young, the tailor, was already fussing over Austin in his usual overzealous manner that many of his patrons adored. Austin seemed to hate every second of it.

"What a strapping man!" Mr. Young exclaimed. "I will have to use twice my fabric for this one!"

He barked a laugh at his own joke and Vincent and Lavender joined in. Austin sneered. "Let us get this over with," he grumbled.

"Oh, no, we cannot rush perfection," Mr. Young said, unperturbed by Austin's attitude. "Miss Latrice asked me to dedicate my entire day to this project and I shan't let her down."

"The entire day?" Austin repeated in shock, giving Lavender a betrayed look.

"Yes, the entire day," Mr. Young reiterated. "Now stand still so that I may take your measurements."

Austin looked just about ready to punch something. Lavender might have been amused by the sight if she wasn't a little afraid that he actually would. She would hate for poor Mr. Young to get caught in the crossfire.

She approached him, grateful that her brother had wandered off to take in one of Mr. Young's bespoke options of waistcoats. "You are scowling," she whispered to Austin.

"How odd. One would think that I do not want to be here."

"Need I remind you that you agreed to this yourself?" Lavender told him. "I did not force you to be here."

He paused for a moment before pushing through gritted teeth, "I am well aware."

"Then I suggest you act like it." He looked sharply at her and Lavender gave him a sweet smile. "You should shave more often. I like it."

Surprise softened his expression. He regarded her for a moment before asking, "How did it go yesterday? I hope you were not in too much trouble with your brother?"

"Vincent cannot stay angry at me for too long, even though he tries his hardest. He was far too preoccupied in a meeting with Colin to scold me much further."

"Colin?" Austin's scowl was back with full force. "Asher?"

"Yes, you met him at the tea party," Lavender reminded him. "When I arrived home, Alice and he were there waiting for me. Apparently, Vincent was so worried that he went to Alice's home to ask her if I had been there and she followed him back to our house to wait for me. Colin was already there to meet with my brother, I believe."

"How convenient," Austin grunted.

Lavender waved it off dismissively. "I'm sure it was about business matters, in which I have no interest. I do not even know when he left. I was too preoccupied talking with Alice about—"

She broke off before she could go any further. Embarrassment washed over her, warming her cheeks, so she pretended to be interested in something else and walked off, leaving Austin in the hands of Mr. Young and his measuring tape.

She approached her brother, looking back at Austin and his uncomfortable stiffness. "Won't you tell me who this mysterious man who claims to be in love with me is?" Lavender asked him.

"I shall not," Vincent answered easily. "But you have very few friends, Lavender. Surely you should be able to figure out who it is."

"None of my friends would ever make such a confession," she said. "You are only saying that to throw me off the scent. It is likely someone I do not know very well."

"Perhaps. Perhaps not."

Lavender sighed. She knew it was foolish hope to try to get that information. But she was only curious. She had no intention of ending this engagement with Austin.

But what would happen if she did? The thought of marrying someone she could care for sounded appealing, even if her quest for revenge had put that thought out of her mind a long time ago. What would happen to Austin if she did? She knew he depended on her family's money to do the repairs of his homes. Would the well run dry if she turned her back on him?

It was none of her concern, she told herself, watching as he reluctantly followed Mr. Youngs's instructions to turn this way and that. He was a grown man, an earl. She was but a young woman who truly did want to start a family after she'd gotten her revenge on Lady Lively. It may be in her best interest to consider what her brother was suggesting.

The thought of doing that left a hole in her chest. The more she thought of it, the bigger the hole grew. Her gaze trailed after Austin as he was led to the changing room with some new waistcoats and breeches given to him by Mr. Young. He was a handsome man, she thought. Even with his reputation, he would fare far better at finding a new match than she did. After all, Lavender knew she was neither pretty nor funny. She was only smart and no man cared to stay long enough to admire such a thing. If there truly was a man out there who loved her, it would be a good idea to give it a chance, wouldn't it?

She'd nearly convinced herself of it, despite how badly it made her feel, when Austin reemerged from the changing room. The moment he did, she forgot about her fears and confusion. She could only see him.

"What do you think?" Mr. Young exclaimed. "Dashing, isn't he? Oh, he could be the Prince Regent himself! It is one of my best works, I assure you."

Lavender said nothing as she studied Austin. He went to a nearby full-length mirror to look at himself. Even she could see that he was a little impressed by what he saw.

"Is this it?" he asked. "Are we done here?"

"Oh, wouldn't you like that?" Mr. Young laughed, clearly unperturbed by Austin's demeanor. "Come now. I have a few more for you to try on and then we are on to picking fabrics!"

"Oh dear God," Austin groaned and it finally broke Lavender out of her haze. She laughed a little louder than she'd planned to, earning the attention of the males in the shop.

"You find this funny, do you?" Austin growled.

She met his eyes unflinchingly, not bothering to grace his words with a response. She only grinned broadly and gestured to the changing room. Mr. Young caught the hint and got into action, ushering Austin inside and telling him to wait there while he fetched a few more things for him to try on.

There was something about the way Austin rolled his eyes to the ceiling, as if calling on God for help, that made her smile widen and all thoughts of ending this engagement left her mind.

Chapter Nineteen

He'd been here for far too long. Austin was all but ready to tear his hair out in frustration. To make matters worse, the energetic tailor didn't seem to be running out of steam any time soon. He always found something else to do, from taking measurements to choosing fabrics to talking about layers.

Austin finally found a break in the entire ordeal after a couple of hours. Mr. Young left him be—though gave him explicit instructions not to leave the shop—while he sorted through design styles with Lavender. They were in a deep discussion about today's fashion, a conversation that Austin was happy they didn't attempt to involve him in. He found a corner of the shop to stew in, to wait until he was dragged back to the center of the room to be primped and prodded all over again.

"It is quite a tedious affair, isn't it?"

Austin grunted in agreement at Vincent's observation. The merchant came to stand next to him, staring at his sister and the tailor.

"Every time Lavender visits Mr. Young, she spends all day and a small fortune," he went on. "I do not know how she has the patience for it."

"Women often love such things," Austin said. "It does not surprise me that she is as thorough with choosing her clothing as she is with everything else."

"Oh? That is quite an observation there, my lord. You seem to have gotten to know Lavender quite well."

"I had no say in the matter. She does make it difficult to hide how headstrong and determined she can be. Otherwise, I never would have set foot in this place in the first place."

Vincent laughed. "I cannot help but agree. My stubborn sister has quite a way of convincing you to do something before you know what you are agreeing to."

"Is that why you came to find me that night?" Austin couldn't help but ask.

"Partially. The truth was that I knew that Lavender needed to be married soon. And as her brother, as her guardian, I was in charge of making that happen. She only exacerbated the urgency by reminding me of her wish to attend this London Season."

"She must be quite pleased with herself then," Austin assumed. Lavender laughed at something Mr. Young said. The sound carried across the room and shaved away some of Austin's ire at being here.

"I'm sure that she is." Vincent paused, shifting from one leg to the other. "But are you, my lord?"

Austin tore his gaze away from Lavender to look at his brother. "Pardon me?"

"I know this is not what you planned for yourself. You only agreed to this for the money. Because of that, I cannot help but think I made a mistake by asking you to do this in the first place."

"I made my decision."

"Yes, you did," Vincent agreed easily. "I shall come right out and say it then. Someone else has asked for Lavender's hand in marriage. Someone who tells me how deeply in love he is with her."

Austin straightened. Without thinking, his gaze fell back on Lavender, who was bent over what looked like a book. A tuft of hair had fallen from its hold and Austin was struck with the urge to cross the shop to tuck it away from her face.

"You are surprised, aren't you?" Vincent went on. "As was I when he approached me. But I began thinking if perhaps coming to you that night might have been a mistake. You do not love my sister. But this man does. Perhaps it would be best for her if she chose him instead."

"Who is this man?" Austin asked, his tone oddly calm despite the unusual sensation coursing through his body.

"Does it matter?" Vincent asked.

Austin paused before he nodded. "Yes."

Vincent frowned at him. Whatever he saw on Austin's face made him sigh and say, "If you must know, it was her friend, Mr. Colin Asher."

He should have known. It had been obvious from the start. Colin Asher had ripped his heart out of his chest and placed it on his sleeve the moment he chased after Lavender at that tea party. Austin was foolish to realize it only now.

He didn't like the black emotion that curled in the pit of his stomach. When he looked back at Lavender, he imagined Colin here instead. Standing next to her, hand on her back, tucking that tuft of hair behind her ear. The thought made him sick.

"You needn't think any further on it," Austin stated coldly. "I have no intention of ending this betrothal."

"If it is the money you want, my lord, I am more than willing to continue to help you adjust your investments and manage your properties so that you will able to take care of it yourself. It is the least I can do for what you have done for Lavender and me so far. You seemed to have made her a little happy in the last few days."

"There isn't any need to. I made a commitment and I shall stick by it."

"Is that the only reason, my lord?" Vincent inquired. "Your commitment?"

Austin did not want to respond that so he didn't. He stalked away from the corner and approached the two, stating that he wanted to try on a few more items. Mr. Young jumped at the chance and Lavender only raised her brows in surprise. He couldn't understand why he did it either. All he knew was that he didn't like the thought of Colin Asher doing a better job at this than he was.

He clung to that thought for the next hour it took for this to be over. By the end of it, Austin was leaving with two new waistcoats and a new pair of breeches. Not to mention a promise for more clothes to arrive over the next few days. He had to admit that when the Latrices spent, they did so without holding back.

Lavender looked rather pleased with herself as they made their way back to the carriage. Austin pictured Colin rushing forward to open the door for her and he found himself doing exactly that without thinking. She frowned at him but said nothing as she climbed in.

"I must say, Austin," she said once they were settled in. "I did not expect you to become so eager by the end of it."

"I was not eager," he explained. "I figured it would end quicker if I was a little less reluctant, that's all."

"A wise thought. But thank you all the same."

"You needn't thank me. I was not the one who spent their money in there."

"Goodness, why don't you accept my gratitude and be done with it?" she said, rolling her eyes.

Did she know how charming she was when she spoke so bossily? Her confidence was one of the most endearing things about her, Austin realized. That and the way her eyes grew smaller as her smile became wider.

"Very well," he mumbled, turning his attention to the window. If he stared at her for too long, he was sure just where his mind would take him.

Despite that, it wasn't long before he was stealing glances. At first, it was because she'd said something and he'd thought she was addressing him. When he realized that she was talking to her brother, Austin turned his eyes out the window. Then it came darting back when she laughed, when she gasped when she spoke with annoyance, and when he thought he might catch her rolling her eyes. She didn't try to engage him in the conversation—probably because he had been so miserable all day—and at first he preferred it that way.

Then he thought of how easily Colin would have been able to integrate himself into the conversation and he didn't like it anymore.

Still, he stayed quiet all the way to their home. He managed to hold his tongue as they all alighted. Vincent was the first to say goodbye. Just as Lavender was about to do the same, Austin stopped her.

"I would like to speak with you for a moment, Lavender," he said earning the surprise of both brother and sister.

Lavender looked back at Vincent and nodded, silently telling him to give them some privacy. Vincent's curiosity kept him lingering for a moment before he turned and walked off.

"What is it?" Lavender asked.

Austin scratched the back of his head. He hadn't thought this all the way through. All he knew was that he didn't want to part ways just yet and had acted on that.

Lavender's frown deepened, eyes tinging with concern. "Is something wrong?"

"No, nothing's wrong," he answered. "I just...don't think I thanked you."

"Thanked me? For what?"

"For doing what you're doing for me." The words were hard to say, even though Austin meant every word of them.

Lavender's expression softened. "You needn't thank me, Austin. I am selfishly thinking about my own needs in all of this, remember?"

"You only want me to believe that."

"And yet it is never truly far from my mind," she said with a laugh. "Well, if there is nothing else…"

"Will you accept me when I come to call you tomorrow?" Austin blurted out.

Lavender blinked. "You...what?"

"It is a simple question," he mumbled, looking away. "I'm sure I needn't repeat myself."

"Yes, you're right. I heard you just fine. I am simply reeling a bit, that's all. Allow me to process it for a moment." Lavender dramatically walked away then began pacing back and forth. She stopped in front of him again after a few seconds, a smile playing around her lips. "What if I say no?"

"Forget I said anything then."

"The answer is yes then," she said quickly before he could turn away. "A surprised and wary yes. But a yes, all the same."

"Are you certain?" he asked. "Are you sure you won't be too busy plotting and scheming?"

Lavender laughed heartily, the sound lifting his spirits. "I shall make some room in my busy schedule for you, Austin."

"Good. Goodbye then."

"Goodbye."

But they didn't part ways right away. They lingered, staring at each other.

Lavender tilted her head to the side and raised her brows, a teasing smile tugging at her lips. Austin felt heat wash over him. Was it...embarrassment? He didn't know and he didn't plan on staying long enough for either one of them to find out. So he gave her a curt nod and climbed back into his carriage. He didn't look out the window until the carriage began to move.

Only then did he allow himself to look back. And she stood there staring after the retreating carriage with that smile on her face. Austin returned it though she was too far to see it.

Chapter Twenty

Lavender wasn't used to acting on impulse, without forethought. She understood the merit in thinking quickly on the spot and usually it worked out in her favor. But charging headfirst into a decision without thinking about it at all was not something she was accustomed to doing.

So the fact that her carriage was pulling up to Austin's townhouse, barely within proper visiting hours, felt a little surreal. The thought had crossed her mind the moment she'd opened her eyes this morning and Lavender hadn't thought twice about going through it with. She hadn't even eaten breakfast. Simply climbed out of bed, gotten ready, and made haste for Austin's home.

Now that she was here, she realized that she might have been a little too hasty. He said that he would come to call on her, after all. She should be waiting for him to follow through with it, not the other way around. What if he was already on his way to see her and they had missed each other?

The thought brought a smile to her face. She doubted it. Austin didn't strike her as the type to wake before noon.

There was still so much she didn't know about him, so many layers to be peeled away before the real Austin was revealed. Excitement unfurled within her as she climbed out of the carriage. It abated when she realized that her carriage was not the only one present.

He had guests? The surly, unsociable Earl of Derby had *guests*?

Lavender simply stood and stared in shock. It didn't seem possible but the carriages bore no crests, while she knew his bore the crest of the earldom. Did it mean that someone else had come to visit him, or perhaps was the carriage waiting to take Austin somewhere?

Lavender made her way to the front door, needing to know for herself. Before long, the anxious butler opened the door for her and all but broke out in cold sweat when he saw who stood before him.

"Good morning," she greeted politely. "I am here to see Lord Derby."

"Ah, I see." He glanced behind him, uncertain. "Lord Derby is preoccupied at the—"

"Are you going to turn me away?" Lavender asked in a firm yet innocent tone. "How odd, considering within a matter of months I will be the mistress of this household."

"Yes, yes, of course, miss." He quickly stepped out of her way, ushering her inside. "I shall inform Lord Derby of your arrival."

He hurried away, leaving Lavender with her question still lingering on her tongue. She supposed she could find out who was here by seeing for herself. She waited impatiently for the butler to return and he stated that she had been invited to join the earl and his guests in the drawing room.

Lavender kept her questions at bay, following behind the butler even though she needed no help in finding the room herself. He opened the door for her and seemed all too eager to leave. Lavender paid the butler no mind as she entered the room.

Out of all the possibilities that had raced through her mind, this was the very last of them. The Countess of Lively sat in the center of the room with a cup of tea in her hands and a smug look on her face. Next to her on the chaise lounge was a young, pretty lady whom Lavender vaguely recognized, though she knew they had never met. And then there was Austin standing by the bay window with his arms crossed looking as if someone had just dashed all his hopes.

Lavender didn't know what to say. So few times had she ever been at a loss for words that it made the silence uncomfortable for a few seconds. She looked at Austin for an explanation but before he could open his mouth, Lady Lively spoke up.

"What a surprise," she purred. "Isn't it a bit too early for you to be here, Miss Lavender? And where is your chaperone?"

Lavender's cheeks grew hot. In her haste to see Austin, she had forgotten to ask Betty to chaperone her. She hadn't expected anyone to be here to witness her social disgrace.

Rather than give the obvious answer, Lavender attempted to deflect with one of her own. "What are you doing here, Lady Lively?"

Lady Lively sipped her tea, a sly smile playing around her lips. She made Lavender wait until she'd returned the teacup to its matching saucer before she said, "Do you know Lady Anna?"

She knew the name and face from afar but... "We have not met."

"She is the daughter of the Marquess of Somerset," Lady Lively stated. "And a lovely lady, I must add. Quite the beauty and has the graces of a princess."

"You flatter me, my lady," Lady Anna spoke. Her voice was light and airy, her cheeks rosy pink. Lavender couldn't deny just how pretty Lady Anna was. Strawberry-blond curls, big brown eyes, and soft perfect lips.

Lavender glanced anxiously at Austin but he was saying nothing, his attention on the two ladies sitting before him, his usual frown on his face. She couldn't tell what he was thinking. Did he think Lady Anna was a beauty as well?

"This, Lady Anna," Lady Lively continued, "is Miss Lavender Latrice. She is the sister of Mr. Vincent Latrice. She is the one I was talking about."

"Oh." Lady Anna giggled softly, eyes glittering with humor. "I see."

Annoyance tinged her confusion. Lavender drew closer, taking the chair directly across from them. To steady her nerves, she poured herself a cup of tea. "I must say that I am surprised, my lady," she said. "I cannot imagine what reason you would have to visit the earl."

"You are not the only one, Lavender," Austin spoke up, his irritation apparent. "These ladies showed up just a few minutes before you did and they are yet to state their reason for coming."

"All things in time, my lord," Lady Lively said easily. "Wouldn't it be nice for us to have a proper conversation first?"

"No," he said. "Out with it."

Lady Lively didn't seem perturbed by his bluntness. Instead, she ran her gaze down the length of him. The first time she did that it had been with disdain and a hint of disgust. This time...was she admiring him?

Lavender looked at Austin as well, noting that he was wearing the new clothes he'd received yesterday. Coupled with his newly-shaven face and his styled hair, he was quite the dashing character. And it seemed both ladies were thinking that as well.

"Very well," Lady Lively went on. "Allow me to be blunt. I came here to introduce Lady Anna to you, my lord."

"And why would I need an introduction?"

"Is that not the first step in starting a friendship? Perhaps more?"

Lavender choked on her tea. She tried to cover it up but she didn't miss the derisive look Lady Lively gave her. Lady Anna's polite and pleasant expression did not move.

"A friendship?" Lavender asked incredulously. "You came all the way here to start a friendship?"

"Yes, to begin with," Lady Lively continued. "You see, my lord, Lady Anna took notice of you at the garden party and thought you were quite fetching. So, since we are acquainted, I thought I could assist in helping you two to get to know each other."

Lavender couldn't believe what she was hearing. She was trying to make a match with a man who was spoken for?

Austin narrowed his eyes at the countess. "Bold of you to do such a thing knowing that I am betrothed to Miss Lavender."

"Yes, yes, so you say. Though I cannot help but wonder how solid such a betrothal is." Lady Lively smiled. "After all, you are yet to announce it in the banns. How can anyone take such a betrothal seriously, if it is not announced?"

"Surely you must be jesting," Lavender murmured, still in disbelief.

"Well, Miss Lavender, this is not something you were meant to hear," Lady Lively said. "But I suppose it is a good thing that you are here. It would be easier for you to know as well."

"For me to know that you mean to take my betrothed?" Lavender murmured.

"An engagement is just one small step, Miss Lavender," Lady Lively stated dismissively. "But the game is not truly over until a wedding occurs, which I hear is months away from now. A lot can happen in that time."

"Ladies." Austin's firm voice kept Lavender from having to think of a response. "I think it is time for you to leave."

"Of course, my lord." Lady Anna stood, planting a perfect smile on her lips. She turned to face Austin, eyes twinkling. "We have overstayed our welcome. I hope we will be able to spend more time together in the future."

Lavender didn't dare look at Austin. She'd seen firsthand how easily men fell for demure and pretty ladies. She didn't want to see it right before her eyes.

She kept her eyes on the table, feeling Lady Lively's eyes boring into her face. Lavender felt the burn of tears at the back of her eyes and she forced them back. She had no reason to cry. Why should she? It was not her fault these ladies thought it fit to try and take her betrothed away from her.

The fact that Austin was not responding right away tore at an opening wound in the center of her chest. He must be reconsidering his options. Trading in the plain, bossy sister of a merchant for the beautiful and wealthy daughter of a marquess.

"My butler will escort you two out," Austin said at last.

Lavender listened as he made his way to the door. Lady Anna moved first, then Lady Lively stood. She didn't have to say anything for her satisfaction to be obvious. As if this meeting had gone exactly the way she had expected it to and knew that there were many more to come.

"It was a pleasure meeting you, my lord," Lady Anna was saying behind Lavender. She still stayed where she sat, shaking.

Austin grunted something Lavender could not hear and soon the ladies were out the door, leaving them alone. Lavender suddenly wished she hadn't come here at all.

***

"Lavender."

She didn't respond to him, her attention out the window. Austin stared at her for a few seconds longer, admiring how lovely she looked this morning. He wanted to say as much to her but he was not sure it was the best thing to do at that moment.

"What do you think of the changes I've made here?" he asked. "Replacing the wallpaper with the same one was your idea but I thought it would be nice to add a few more artistic pieces as well."

"Hm." She didn't look back at him. From the moment Lady Lively and Lady Anna left, Lavender had stood and made her way over to the window. Minutes had gone by and she was yet to say a word.

Austin scratched the back of his head, not knowing what to say. That entire conversation had been nothing short of uncomfortable. Austin had considered sending them away when his butler had announced their visit and had only accepted their call when he thought that it might be able to help Lavender. He didn't think that it would turn into...that.

"What are you doing here?" he asked after a few more moments of silence.

"Why?" she snapped without looking at him. "Were you hoping to have some more time alone with Lady Anna?"

"Of course not," he answered easily, a little confused as to why she would think such a thing. "But when we parted ways yesterday, it was on the agreement that I would come to call on you. Not the other way around."

"I made a mistake, it seemed," she mumbled.

"Lavender." Austin sighed. He didn't know how to fix this. He didn't even know what he was fixing. So he tried to distract her. "The art pieces. Do you like them?"

"Yes," she answered.

"You have not even looked."

Lavender didn't say anything for a moment before turning to look at him. Austin pointed to the mantle. There, next to the portrait of his stepmother was one of his late father. He had rummaged through his father's old things and thought it would be a nice addition to the drawing room, as per Lavender's suggestion.

Her expression hardly changed as she took it in. "That's nice," she answered noncommittally.

Austin stifled his sigh. "I have a few more changes that I would like to show you. And I do need your input on what other renovations I should do."

Lavender shook her head. She turned away from the window to face him. "Perhaps I should just leave. I am in no mood to talk about such things and I will be terrible company."

She attempted to do just that. Austin stepped in her path before she could make it to the door. "What is the matter, Lavender?" he asked, sounding a little weary.

Fire flashed behind her brown eyes. "What is the matter?" she repeated. "Surely you do not think I would be fine after hearing such a thing?"

"That was a bit outrageous of them to do, I agree. But you needn't be bothered by the sayings of an egotistical countess and her lackey."

"Is that so?" She crossed her arms, face flaring with anger and something else Austin could not name. The anger, however, he could respond to. Anger he was used to. "You mean for me to stand here and talk about renovations with you when it is clear that you could trade me in for another lady at any moment."

Austin scoffed. "Do you really think so lowly of me to think I would give a damn about a title? Surely you must know me better by now."

"It is not so much the title as it is the benefits that comes with it. It is obvious, Austin. Lady Anna is the daughter of a marquess and likely possesses a dowry that will be more than enough for you to attain all your goals. Not to mention the fact that she is far more—"

She broke off, turning away.

"Far more what?" Austin pressed.

"It's nothing. Let us forget it. I suppose I cannot blame you if you make such a decision, all things considered."

"Lavender, this is silly."

"Of course you would think so," she mumbled. When she faced him again, Austin could have sworn he saw the faint sheen of tears in her eyes. She blinked and it was gone. "I am in no mood to continue the conversation. I should leave."

She attempted to pass him again but he caught her wrist gently. "You don't have to go, Lavender. Don't let those ladies ruin your days."

"If you think it is just the ladies, Austin, then you should think again." She calmly pried her wrist away from him and walked away.

Austin wanted to chase after her. He would have, if he knew what to say to her. Frustration mounted in him with every step she took away from him and once he was alone in the drawing room, he let out a long breath.

He'd just made that situation worse, he realized. And as usual, he hadn't a clue how to fix it.

Chapter Twenty-One

It didn't take him long to realize that he couldn't stay in the house stewing in his frustration any longer. Austin tried drinking something stronger than tea and it didn't work. He paced around the house, barking nonsensical orders at his servants but that only worsened his mood, thinking about how disapproving Lavender would be if she saw him doing such a thing. By midday, he couldn't handle it any longer and set course for the only place he could go to work off this anxious energy.

Had it been under the cover of nighttime, he would have gone straight to the docks. But since it was still during the light of day, Austin went to an old home in west London instead.

The house had once belonged to a baron who had lost his fortune to gambling. Austin didn't know what had happened to the baron. All he knew was that the debts he'd incurred had made him quite a few enemies. A few of those enemies had chased him out of London. Others had taken his home and turned it into a den of sorts.

All sorts of shady characters came and went from this place. Austin had discovered it after he'd left university and had fallen in with a rough crowd out of rebellion to his father and stepmother. Since accepting the title, he thought that he would leave this life behind. But he supposed he was used to falling back into old habits once emotions ran high.

And his emotions were out of control.

He didn't understand Lavender at all. He thought she would be pleased that he had invited Lady Lively into his home when she'd come to call on him. Albeit, he didn't think that the conversation would turn to that but how was that his fault? Why would she think he deserved any of her anger?

Austin couldn't understand it. And because he couldn't understand it, he wanted to forget about it. And since he could not get Lavender and that look in her eyes before she'd left out of his head no matter how hard he tried, Austin sought distraction instead.

None of the men lingering in the yard of the den stopped him as he sauntered by. He had a bit of a name to these men. Ruthless, determined. Austin had always lived as if his life was dispensable and it had earned him a reputation that wasn't easily shaken.

He entered and ignored the other men lounging about. These were men who had nothing better to do with their time than to plot and fight. Men from poor families, men from wealthy backgrounds looking for a tougher life. Walks of life that he shouldn't be caught dead with. If Lavender knew he was here…

Austin shook his head, trying to banish her from his mind. It was easier said than done.

He made his way to the dining room. It looked the exact same as he'd last seen it. Most of the furniture had been cleared from the room and the art pieces had been sold a long time ago. In the center of the room, two men tussled with each other, while other men shouted around them. Austin ignored them, making his way to the left of the room.

"Well, would you look at this?" The lanky man lounged in a chair with his arm slung over the back of it. He was the only one with a chair. Everyone else leaned against the wall or sat on the floor. "I didn't think I would live to see you walk back in here."

"Never far from my mind," Austin murmured, though it wasn't quite true. He hadn't thought about fighting since…well since he met Lavender.

"I suppose you cannot really take the fighter out of the man, even if you slap a title on his name." The lanky man stood. He went by the name Sprout and had a reputation that earned him fear from nearly anyone who'd heard of him. One would never think that he was actually the third son of the Duke of Harrington.

Sprout had told Austin that in confidence and Austin never cared to tell anyone about his secret. Now that he looked at him though, he found it a bit amusing that discarded or ignored men of the ton usually ended up in the same place. He wondered how many others here were from titled families.

"I want a fight," Austin stated.

"And a fight you will have." Sprout shot from his chair. "Oi! Clear out!"

The two men who had been unsuccessfully trying to get the upper hand on each other followed the command quickly. They scrambled to their feet and hurried away from the middle of the room.

Austin went to take their place. In the corner of his eye, he saw Sprout shove someone else into the middle. The man who would now be his opponent had scars all over his arms and was already sporting a fading bruise under his eye.

It reminded Austin of the look of horror on Lavender's face when he'd shown up to the tea party with his face bruised. Would she be upset if he did that again?

The answer came quickly even as the man threw the first punch. She would be upset. Perhaps it wasn't a good idea to risk that again.

Austin dodged the punch and threw one into the man's midsection. The feel of his knuckles colliding with flesh took the edge off. Austin would just have to make sure that he didn't get punched in his face. Easy.

As soon as the thought crossed his mind, the man recovered far quicker than Austin expected and rammed his elbow into Austin's chin. Austin's head snapped back, stars filling his vision. But he was aware enough to dodge the kick aimed for his side. He caught another one, slamming his elbow on the man's knee and shoving him back onto the floor.

His opponent was large and absorbed hits as if they were nothing. Nothing kept him down for long. Every blow Austin dealt felt as if he was hitting an unmoving wall that was all too eager to hit him back. Before long his attempt to keep his face bruise-free had failed. His entire body would be covered in bruises, his nose bleeding, and hopefully not broken.

Austin kept coming back up, though. Even though he was taking a beating, he was giving one as well. And that was exactly what he needed, something to punch over and over again until his frustrations surrounding Lavender was gone. Every time he took a blow though, he saw her face. He saw her horror. Her worry.

Perhaps this was not a good idea.

The realization came a little too late, he realized, as he blocked a blow with his forearm and felt the force of it rock through his body. He had to end this quickly before it got any further.

Austin took another blow to the chin to keep his opponent close. Then he caught his arm, swinging him around until he forced the man to his knees. Without giving him the chance to pull free, he rammed his fist into his jaw hard enough to knock him out cold.

Applause ran through the room but Austin ignored it. He didn't bother to say goodbye to Sprout or anyone else. He simply stalked out of the room, feeling worse now than he had been before. Outside, he spat blood into the grass and climbed into his carriage, a little grateful he hadn't sent his coachman away like he usually did.

His entire body ached. How could he have thought that would make him feel better? Now Lavender would only look at him like a monster when they went to the horse racing.

He shouldn't care. He was only doing this to fulfill his side of the contract, after all. It mattered not what she thought of him.

Austin didn't like how much it felt as if he was lying to himself.

As soon as he returned to the townhouse, he ordered his butler to fetch him his decanter and glass and bring it to his bedchamber. If fighting didn't help then he would simply drink the rest of the day away.

"This came for you when you were away, my lord," his butler told him, handing him a letter.

Austin was about to send him away, telling him he was in no mood to receive any correspondence, but then he noticed Lavender's hasty handwriting.

Austin quickly unfolded the letter. His mood soured with every word he read. After all that happened, Lavender had decided to invite Colin Asher to attend the horse races with them? Hadn't she added that to their events because of him? Why would she want to bring another gentleman in the middle of that?

There was no hope for his mood to improve today. That letter had only made things worse. Austin tossed it aside and turned to make his way out the door, heading to White's instead. Maybe that would be enough to fix this.

***

The moment Austin walked into White's, he spotted Colin Asher occupying one of the tables at the far back of the gentleman's club. And as soon as he saw Colin, Austin's frustration with the situation he found himself in culminated in a ripe, tasty need for revenge.

He stalked forward, hands curled into fists at his side. Men watched him go by and whispers followed in his wake. The look in his eye had everyone parting ways, not daring to stay in his path. He must have looked rather formidable but when he arrived at Colin's table, the other man merely looked up at him with nothing but disdain.

"Get up," Austin ordered. "We need to talk."

Colin snorted derisively. "You do not order me about, lord," he hissed. "And seeing the state you're in, I would think that you had much better things to do than to frequent my watering hole."

Austin gave him an ugly smile. Colin's response was exactly how he wanted it to be. Tense and hostile enough for whatever was about to come to feel necessary.

He caught the lapels of the man sitting across from Colin and hauled him out of the armchair. The man did not so much as protest. Austin claimed the chair, fixing Colin with a glare.

"I thought you men had more respect than this," he growled. "To think a mere bastard understood the gentlemanly rules of society far better than you do."

Colin tilted his head to the side, narrowing his eyes. "I'm afraid I do not know what you are talking about."

"I'm certain that you do," Austin countered. "Lavender."

Colin reached for his drink in an idle manner that increased Austin's annoyance. As if he had no reason to be afraid of the bruised man before him itching for another fight. "Yes, Lavender. My closest and oldest friend. She has always been too nice for her own good. I figure that must be the reason why she's taken pity on a man like yourself and has accepted your sad proposal."

"And because of that, you think it proper to ask for her hand in marriage when you know she is meant for another."

Murmurs rushed through the club as the onlookers reeled in surprise. Colin hardly flinched. "It was about time I made my move. I was waiting for the right time, but you took that from me."

"Back down, Asher."

"Or what?" Colin leaned forward, his stare icy. "Do not think I am unaware of the fact that you are only marrying Lavender for her wealth, Derby. Forgive me if I do not think she should be a pawn to save you from the mismanagement of your own."

"You haven't a clue what Lavender and I have," Austin stated. He ignored the voice in the back of his head that said he didn't know what they had either. "And it shouldn't matter to you. If I find out you are still sniffing around her like the hound you are, then I will ensure that you regret it."

"You do not frighten me. You may hold a title but at the end of it, you are still the son of a maid and nothing more." He sneered, his handsome features twisting into something grotesque. "I may not have a title but I am of finer breeding stock than you could ever be. I am good for Lavender while you...you are nothing but a leech looking for something to suck on. I won't allow it."

Austin barked a harsh, unamused laugh. "Choice words coming from the man who is yet to say any of this to Lavender herself. What would happen if you did, Asher? Are you afraid that she will do exactly what we all expect her to do, which is to reject you soundly and send you on your way?"

Austin struck a nerve with that one. He saw the shutters of anger that came down over Colin's face. "Everyone knows that I am the best match for her. I know it. Our peers know it. Indeed, even her brother knows. Lavender is smart enough to realise it herself as well."

"I wish you all the luck with that one." Austin stared him down for a few seconds, wanting to do more. He would have lunged across the table and pummeled his head into the wall just for the mere fact that he'd dared to insult him. Austin didn't quite know when he had changed but all he could hear was Lavender's disapproving voice in his head.

That was the only reason he stood, deciding to walk away from this. She would not like it if he were to attack her friend, warranted or not. He didn't need to give her another reason to be upset.

Just as he turned away, Colin said, "That's right, Derby. Walk away like you should have from the very beginning. Once Lavender and I are wed, perhaps you could forget about how horribly you've embarrassed yourself."

Austin paused. Colin was dangling bait in front of Austin's face—whether he knew it or not—and Austin was tempted to grab ahold of it. Instead, he said, "You're a sad man if you think that will happen."

"Lavender has always been in love with me, Derby. She just hasn't realised it yet."

The memory of Lavender and Colin standing in that hallway at the Lawrence residence staring at each other flashed through Austin's mind. At the time, it had felt uncomfortably like he had walked in on something private. It had bothered him then and bothered him even more now.

Peace be damned, he thought as he turned and stalked back to the table. The satisfaction that had shone in Colin's eyes turned to panic when Austin seized by the collar and drew him to his feet.

"Fight me," he growled. "Prove your love once and for all."

Colin paled. He glanced around him, noting the watching eyes of everyone nearby. Austin knew he wouldn't back down. It was socially disgraceful to do so when challenged to a duel and Austin, for the first time, was happy to live up to society's expectations.

"Very well." Colin shoved Austin back and Austin allowed him. The gentlemen nearby began to clear the tables and chairs away, giving them the space they needed for their duel. Colin looked Austin up and down and smirked. "Although I think it would be unfair of me to fight you in such a state."

"If you think so, Asher," Austin said. He was tired of words now. He wanted action. He wanted this man to see that it wouldn't be so easy to take what was his.

Austin didn't usually like to take the first swing. He preferred to stay on the defensive until he got a good feel of his opponent. Then he attacked relentlessly until he knew they could go no further.

Fighting Colin Asher was no different. He had no experience, no skill. He knew how to throw a punch well enough but was sloppy enough that every single one of them missed. Austin danced around him, watching as he threw his entire body weight into every punch and kick he doled out, watching his frustration mount when he couldn't land a hit.

At last, Austin struck. Colin's head snapped back from the blow, blood trickling to his lips. He snarled and charged again but his anger only made him unsteady on his feet. With one quick sidestep, Austin swept Colin's legs from underneath him and he fell to the floor.

Gentlemen roared around them, urging them on. It was an easy fight, an easy win. Austin dodged a few more of Colin's desperate punches and doled out a few of his own. Colin's jaw, his ribs, his stomach. Hard enough for him to feel it the next morning.

But when he punched him again, hearing a crack, reality came crashing down on him.

Lavender was going to hate him for this. No matter how Austin felt about him, Colin was still her friend. And she would be very unhappy if this altercation brought on a scandal.

Austin saw his winning chance but hesitated. Colin stepped in as if he sensed it and rammed his fist into Austin's jaw with all his might. That moment of uncertainty was all it took, Austin realized.

At first, the world spun. Then splotches of darkness swam his vision. And the last thing he saw before he fell unconscious was Colin's victorious grin.

Chapter Twenty-Two

It was the day of the horse racing and Lavender felt...off. She couldn't put her finger on it. From the moment she woke up, there was an unsettling feeling simmering in the pit of her stomach telling her that something was wrong.

She tried to ignore it, wrote it off as anxiousness. After all, she was likely to see many influential members of the ton at this event. She might even see Lady Lively herself, since she was known to frequent the horse races now and again. After their last encounter, Lavender wanted to ensure that everything was absolutely perfect this time.

Despite that, she could not shake the feeling that something bad was about to happen.

Thankfully, she was able to ignore the feeling as best as she could until the time came for her to get ready. She chose her dress perfectly, matching it with her bonnet and gloves. Her hair was simply done in a small chignon with a few loose curls framing her face. She opted to carry her reticule even though she had no intentions of spending any money, needing to put her fan in something.

And then she waited. And waited. Austin was supposed to come for her, since it would be ideal for them to arrive in a carriage bearing his crest. And yet he seemed like he was late yet again.

As the minutes wore on, Lavender's impatience grew into frustration. She should have known better than to have trusted him to do this. But she thought that they had crossed over into more familiar territory after she'd spent the night at his townhouse. She thought that, after she'd told him how important this all was to her, that he would have made an effort. Surely he wasn't doing this because of the way they'd parted ways yesterday?

She stood, shaking with frustration. She would just go to him then. There was no way she would allow him to embarrass her once more.

Lavender marched out of the drawing room. As soon as she stepped into the foyer, she halted in surprise. "Colin? What are you doing here?" Lavender eyes widened as she took him in. "And what in heaven's name happened to your face?"

He was quite the sight. His alabaster skin now sported blackening bruises across his nose, his jaw and one entire eye. As he came forward, Lavender saw that his upper lip had been split open as well.

"Were you in a fight?" she gasped. "Who did this to you?"

Despite the sorry state he was in, Colin still managed a smile. "My, Lavender, it has been quite a while since you've worried for me like this."

"Enough of the jests, Colin." Unable to help herself, she reached out and brushed her fingers across the bruise spreading across the cheek. He flinched. "This is horrible. Has a physician looked at you yet?"

"Yes, and I believe that the worse has passed. It is quite painful, though. Despite that, I thought that I could not leave you all by yourself on this day."

Lavender frowned. "I am not alone. Austin will be coming to fetch me for the races."

"I think he is a little...preoccupied."

"What do you mean?"

Colin's expression softened. He opened his mouth to speak but then his eyes fluttered and he swayed on his feet for a moment. Lavender panicked, wrapping her arms around him even though she doubted she would be able to break his fall if he were to fall unconscious on the spot. They would simple topple to the floor together.

Even so, he immediately leaned against her, murmuring, "Forgive me, I...I just need to sit down for a moment."

"Of course. Do you think you can make it to the drawing room?"

"If you help me."

Lavender didn't hesitate to slide her arm around his waist. Colin instantly rested nearly his entire body weight on her and she had to adjust herself to keep from tipping over. Slowly, with his head on her shoulder and her arm trying desperately to hold him upright, Lavender helped him to the drawing room.

He collapsed into the nearest armchair and rested his head on the back of the chair. "Forgive me, Lavender. This was not my intention."

"Getting beaten to a pulp?" she tried to jest.

His eyes shot open and she caught a flash of irritation. "I was not beaten to a pulp. My opponent fared far worse, I assure you."

Lavender didn't bother to point out that she was only trying to lift his spirits by joking. She sat on the chaise lounge across from him with a frown. "What happened, Colin?"

"It...it isn't anything serious. Just know that I am fine and quite capable of escorting you to the races."

"But I do not need an escort. I will be attending with Austin, if you recall. I was supposed to meet Alice and you there."

"I do not think your betrothed will be able to come," he said, his tone a tad bitter. "After all, it is way past the time for you to leave and yet he is nowhere to be found."

Lavender hated how right he was about that. Still, she felt the need to defend him. "There must be something keeping him. I shall wait here a while longer for him to show. You're welcome to rest here for a bit more and then head there yourself."

Colin sat up, fixing her with a stern glare. "Lavender, you are far too smart to make excuses for him like that. You know as well as I that he has no intention of showing."

"I know no such thing."

"Then I suppose you are not aware of the fact that he has gone back to his previous lifestyle of drinking and gambling the night away. Last I heard, Lav, he had quite a rough night trying to win back the money he has lost."

Lavender blinked. That didn't sound right. Even though Colin was the one saying it, even though she had no reason to doubt anything her friend said to her, Lavender simply could not believe that the reason why Austin was not here was because he was too inebriated from his night of drinking and gambling. She felt her heart cracking at the mere thought of it.

But the longer those words sat between them, the more believable they became. After all, Austin had made it no secret that he enjoyed less honorable pasttimes. What if much of his mismanagement of funds stemmed from his love of gambling in the first place? He'd never said as much to her before but...Colin wouldn't lie to her, would he?

Colin moved, slipping out of his chair and next to her with such grace that she almost forgot that he had been dizzy just moments before. He took her hand without warning, capturing it in both of his own.

"I warned you about him, didn't I?" he said softly. "I told you that he was not the kind of man you want to be attached to. My only wish is for you to see the truth of who he is before it is too late."

Lavender frowned slightly, searching Colin's eyes. Perhaps it was because of her own growing feelings for Austin but she noticed something that she'd never seen previously before. Something shone back at her, something she should have realised a long time ago.

All of a sudden, Vincent's words came rushing back to her.

Lavender's heart slowed as she asked, as calmly as she could, "Did you ask Vincent for my hand in marriage, Colin?"

Colin blinked in surprise. And then his gaze soften, a smile tugging at his lips. Lavender could not return it. It felt as if a bucket of cold water had just been dumped all over her.

"I thought I was being romantic by asking him first," he said, brushing his thumb over the back of her hand. She would have pulled her hand free had she not been frozen in shock. "When you revealed that you were betrothed to the Earl of Derby, I knew I had to act. I realised that I might have waited a little too long to reveal my feelings and I did not want lose my chance."

"Colin..."

He shifted closer, until their arms brushed. "Lavender, I am helplessly in love with you. I have been for as long as I can remember and I had hoped that you would recognise my feelings. Now I know that I must say it boldly and loudly for you to know. I love you, Lavender. And it is my wish for us to spend the rest of our days married and happy with each other."

"Colin..." Lavender didn't allow herself to look away from him as she forced out her next to word. "No."

Colin jerked in shock. "No?" he echoed. "What do you mean, no?"

"Exactly that, Colin." She pulled her hand free. He looked down at them as if it were an act of betrayal. "I love you dearly but only as a friend. I feel no romantic feelings towards you nor do I believe that I will."

"Do you love the earl then?"

She didn't want to answer that. She didn't think now was the time to explore such a thing. She only shook her head and said, "You should go on to the races. Or perhaps, if you are still feeling dizzy, you should go home and get some rest."

"No." Colin got to his feet, running his hand over his face. Lavender watched as he paced back and forth now and again before turning back to face her. "I accept what you have said. For now. I will still choose to believe, however, that you will come to fall for me in time."

"Colin…"

"And the truth of the matter is that your betrothed is late. If you wait here any longer for him, so will you be. I shall escort you to the races." After a beat, he added, "I hear that Lady Lively will be in attendance this afternoon as well."

Lavender thinned her lips. The truth was that she did not want to be late. She'd planned this out too meticulously to be comfortable with everything not completely going her way. It bothered her that Austin did not respect her enough to follow through with his promises.

A horrible thought whispered through her mind. Perhaps he would rather spend time with a beautiful, demure lady who would not pressure him to attend such things? Was he already pulling away from her to make his way to the marquess' daughter?

Jealousy seized her so soundly that Lavender was at a loss for words for a moment. Her mind was beginning to spiral. She'd never deemed herself an insecure lady and yet here she was comparing herself to a lady she hardly knew!

"Come." Colin was upon her again, taking her hand. This time, he pulled her to a stand. "Let us go and enjoy ourselves. We can forget about everything that was just said."

That's easier said than done, she wanted to say. But she didn't say anything, not pulling away as he led her to the door, even though she wanted to.

She supposed it would not be too bad to go with Colin. Austin clearly did not plan on showing up. Lavender refused to sit here and wait around for him, even though the thought of being abandoned by him tore an irreparable hole in her chest. It was a hole she would ignore for now. A hole that would not stop her from carrying out her plan.

Lavender nodded quietly to herself, resigning to attending the races with Colin.

But before they could take another step, the door opened.

Austin came limping in on a cane.

Chapter Twenty-Three

If he felt like collapsing before, it was nothing compared to walking into the drawing room of Latrice Manor and seeing the man who had put him in this state holding the hand of his betrothed.

For a second that felt far too long, Austin had to stifle the rage that choked him. He wanted to march forward and snatch her away from him, to put an end to this vicious cycle of jealousy he felt whenever Colin Asher was near.

But he was no in state to do such a thing. He woke up in a back room of White's with a splitting headache and stars dancing before his vision. He didn't know who had been there at the time, only that they had informed him of the fact that it was the next day and that it was best that he remained on bedrest. All Austin could think was that he had to get to Lavender. That Lavender was waiting for him.

He didn't think he would show up to see him here.

"Austin!" Lavender gasped. She pulled away from Colin despite the look of displeasure on his face and hurried to Austin's side. "My goodness, what happened to you?"

Austin held on tightly to his cane. He couldn't even remember where he'd gotten it. Perhaps the man who had helped him at White's had given it to him considering the fact that his heavy head made it difficult to walk straight.

He grunted something, leaning in as Lavender opened her arms to him. She barely managed to stay on her feet as his entire body weight collapsed on to her. Austin struggled to lean away, keeping his eyes open.

"Oh, Derby, you should be home. Go and see a physician, for your sake."

"Colin, hush!" Lavender hissed before Austin could think of a retort. She smelled glorious as usual. And her hair felt softer than ever against his cheek. "Come, Austin, sit right here."

Lavender held on to him as she guided him to an armchair. The moment Austin sank into the comfortable seating he had to remind himself to keep his eyes open. He'd been knocked unconscious enough times to know when he was concussed.

He didn't say as much to Lavender. He focused on her face, oddly touched by the worry written into every bit of it.

"What happened to you?" Lavender asked, sinking to his side. "Were you fighting again?"

"Does it not look like it?" he couldn't help but say. When she scowled at him, he forced a smile on his face. "Forgive me. I suppose this is no time for jests."

"Yes, I am in no mood for laughing," she chastised. "Tell me why you are in this state. And why are you here instead of home receiving care from your physician?"

"Because I thought it more important to come here." With the hand not gripping his cane reached out to brush her cheek. "You were waiting for me, weren't you?"

Despite the slight blush that touched her cheeks, her glare did not lift. "So what? Your health is more important, is it not? I should call my physician since you are too stubborn to get any medical assistance."

She began to rise but he caught her wrist. "Don't. We have go to the races. For your plan."

"Forget about the plan! Look at you!" Hysteria tinged her voice. Even so, she didn't pull away from him, sinking to his side once more. "You're bruised all over and you cannot walk without a cane. How could you let this happen to you? Did you try to win back the money you lost last night?"

That made him frown. "Lost? Do you think I was out gambling?"

"Wasn't that what you were doing?" she asked, confused.

Before he could respond, Colin cut in. "Don't be a fool, Derby. You're clearly in no state to attend anything. You cannot even stand. If you're worried about Lavender, then there is no need to be. She is in good hands."

Austin lifted his eyes to meet his. "Is that so? And I suppose she got the idea that I was gambling from you as well."

"Would you rather I tell her the truth?"

"What do you mean?" Lavender cut in, looking between the two men. "What is the truth?"

Neither one of them spoke. Austin didn't want to tell her, didn't want to face her wrath when she heard that he had picked a fight with her friend and possibly caused an irreparable scandal. And he could tell Colin did not want to either, though he wasn't entirely certain of his reason for holding back the truth.

They stood at a stalemate, neither one of them saying anything. Austin could feel Lavender's mounting frustration. "One of you had better tell me the truth of what is going on or so help me," she warned.

Austin saw when Colin cracked. He opened his mouth, wanting to get the truth out before Colin did. But then the door opened and Vincent stalked in looking furious.

His eyes were fixed on Austin. He marched forward, grabbing Austin by the front of his waistcoat and hauling him to his feet. "Are you out of your mind, Lord Derby?" he bellowed.

"Vincent, what are you doing?" Lavender screamed. "Let him go right now! He is injured!"

Vincent didn't move. He continued glaring into Austin's face and, in the state that he was, Austin could do nothing but stare back. Lavender pushed her small frame between them, forcing her brother back. As soon as Vincent let him go, she caught Austin as best as she could and helped him back into the chair. Then she whirled on her brother.

"What has gotten into you?" she demanded, crossing her arm and standing in front of Austin like a guard dog.

"How funny, Lav, because I have the same question for the earl," Vincent spat. He looked at Colin and it seemed to upset him even more. He pinched the bridge of his nose and drew in a long breath. "If you two decided to fight each other in public then the least you could have done was stay in your homes rather than take your issues here, to my sister."

Austin stared into Lavender's back. He watched her go rigid, watched as she looked at Colin then turned to look down on him. Confusion was written across her face, disbelief in her brown eyes even though he could tell that she was starting to put the pieces together.

"You two did this to each other?" she asked both of them at the same time.

"It is the talk around town, Lav," her seething brother informed her. "Apparently, Austin approached Colin at White's Gentleman's Club and, after a heated argument, decided that it would best for them to settle it with fists. Which is why this one looks black and blue," he pointed to Colin, "and this one cannot stand or walk without a cane," he ended with Austin.

Lavender shook her head. "There must be a reason."

"There is no reason other than the fact that the earl is nothing but a brute! I heard that he was the one who incited the fight. And given everything I knew about him—which was far too little, I'll admit—I should have known better than to entrust you to a man like him, Lavender."

"Vincent." Lavender seemed to be struggling on her own with the truth. Austin could say nothing. He'd felt shame from the moment he woke up from his unconscious state but it did not choke him as soundly as it did now. "Let's calm down."

"I will not calm down, Lavender! It is one thing for him to carry the reputation of a brute and a bastard but it is another thing entirely for him to live up to one." He whirled on Austin. "I shall give you anything you want to break our contract. Money is no issue here. As long as you leave."

"Contract?" Colin spoke up. "You are contracted to marry her?"

Lavender mimicked her brother by pinching the bridge of her nose. "Colin, please."

Austin didn't look away from Vincent. He deserved this. Every bit of anger and disappointment directed towards him was duly sent. But he would not back down. "I made a promise by signing that contract. I shall not break it."

"You made a promise because money is what you wanted," Vincent reminded him. "I shall give you what you want, so long as you leave my sister be. I shall find a better husband for her."

"Money was what I wanted," Austin answered calmly. "It is no longer my motivation."

"And what do you mean by that?"

Austin did not answer. He knew the truth deep down. Perhaps it was being knocked upside the chin that brought him to his senses. But before he could find the right words, Lavender stepped in between them once again.

"Vincent, enough. I understand that you're angry but there must have been a reason why Austin and Colin fought. Austin is not an irrational man. Whatever drove him do such a thing must have been worth it." Lavender glanced uncertainly at him. "Wasn't it?"

He met her eyes, hoping she could see the depth of his earnestness as he said, "Yes, it was. We fought over you, Lavender. And it was certainly worth it."

Chapter Twenty-Four

Lavender only stared at him for a long moment. She could see him fighting the unconsciousness but the shock his words induced made it difficult to remember that he should be in bed under the care of a physician and not here talking about this.

"Over me?" she repeated dumbly. She didn't realize she'd sank to his side again until he had to shift his head to look down at her. "I don't...I don't understand."

"Ignore his ramblings, Lavender," Colin spoke up from behind her. "He is delirious and clearly does not know what he is saying."

"Do you call him a liar then?" Lavender asked, her tone sharp. She turned her head, looking at Colin from the corner of her eye. "And my brother as well? And all the others who have begun to spread rumours of your duel?"

She saw him scratch the back of his head. "I did not mean it that way."

She turned back to Austin. His eyes were fluttering and he was holding his cane so tightly that his knuckles turned white. "Leave us be," she said. "You as well, Vincent. I want to speak with Austin alone."

"I'll be damned if I leave you alone with this—"

"But you would much rather entertain the thought of me marrying someone who claims he is in love with me?" she snapped at her brother, cutting him off. Lavender stood and whirled on him. "Someone who claims he is my friend yet sneakily came here knowing what he did last night and lied to my face about it?"

To her left, Colin made a step toward. "Lavender, you know that wasn't my—"

"Leave!" she shouted, her voice so loud that even Vincent jumped. "I said I need to speak with Austin alone."

Vincent seemed reluctant. But he knew he couldn't argue with her, not when she was like this. And especially not when it was clear that she was right. He shot an uncertain glance at Austin and then at Colin. Despite colorful bruises on Colin's face, Lavender had never seen it paler.

After a few seconds, they finally gave in and sluggishly made their way to the door. Lavender turned to watch them go, crossing her arms. She did not let up her glare until the door closed behind them.

Once they were gone, her anger fell away, leaving the aching worry open like a pulsing wound. She was by Austin's side again in a second. "I'm going to call you a physician," she told him. "For now, just rest until they get here. Close your eyes."

He shook his head weakly. "That isn't a good idea," he murmured.

"Why?" Lavender didn't know what else to do. It was alarming watching the tough, burly earl appear so weak and fragile. Panic settled into the rhythms of her heartbeat, chasing away all the questions she had. She leaned forward, pressing a hand against his forehead. He wasn't hot yet his eyes fluttered as if he was being taken by a fever dream.

Slowly, Austin reached up and took her hand. She thought that he would move it away but he just cradled it to his chest. "You have questions," he said softly.

She nodded. Tears rushed to her eyes. She wanted so badly to get up and get him help but she remained there, trapped with her hand against his chest. "Quite a few. But I don't think now is the time to ask them."

"Allow me to guess what they are then," he said. "You want to know why we fought over you."

She bit her lip, nodding.

"You're a smart woman, Lav," he said. "I'm sure you must have drawn your own conclusion by now."

"It would only be fair if you said it. I would rather not assume."

He nodded. The action seemed to cause him some pain. "That is true. Perhaps I should have used what little strength I had left to tell you that first, rather than arguing with Asher and your brother."

"Austin." The grip on her hand grew weak. His fluttering eyelids began to slow as his eyes slowly closed. Her panic shot to her throat, tears streaming down her cheeks. "Austin?"

He didn't respond. He closed his eyes and let out one long breath.

She had read of such things before. Of men who had been hit so squarely in the head that they held no hope of staying alive. And even if they did, they were only half their former selves, their brains damaged to the point of no return. As she watched Austin's body sink deeper into the chair, the cane falling from his now loose hand, Lavender thought that those fears had been realized.

What happened next felt like a blur. She did not remember shooting to her feet, only that she was suddenly outside of the drawing room, running right into Vincent who had been waiting on the other side. She barely got the words out but he understood. His previous anger was gone. Only firm determination and action. He got into action, holding her tightly as he sent for the physician.

Somehow, she took notice of the fact that Colin was still there. But he didn't step forward to comfort her. He only watched from afar as she buried her face into Vincent's shoulder and wailed. Knees buckling, throat hoarse, she could only recall Austin's long breath and her panic transformed into something she could no longer contain.

She always thought she worked well under pressure. But this was something else entirely. Horror and grief trapped her so soundly that Lavender was hardly aware of what was going on around her. Vincent must have ordered footmen to get Austin. She watched him being carried by three men and followed without hesitation, even though the sight of his lifeless body was like a million knives piercing him at once.

They brought him to one of the guest bedchambers and laid him gently on the bed. She threw herself to the side of the bed, seizing one hand in both of her own. She bent her head and prayed and cried. Lavender didn't know how long she stayed there. Only that eventually, Vincent came to pry her away from the room because the physician had arrived.

Her brother stayed by her side, holding her as she cried. Colin was nowhere to be found. Perhaps he was in another room or had decided to leave. She didn't care. She didn't care about anything other than the fact that she had made a dreadful decision in not sending for the physician the moment she saw Austin's state. She would have been able to stop this from happening. She would have been able to prevent his...

"He'll be all right," Vincent soothed her. He'd been saying that for a while now, she realized. They sat outside the bedchamber on the floor, his hand slowly stroking her hair. "Everything will be all right."

"I love him, Vincent," Lavender managed to say. Her throat felt raw and painful but she needed to say the words aloud. She needed someone else to know if it couldn't be Austin.

Vincent was quiet for a very long time. Then he said, "In that case, he has no choice but to get better."

Lavender silently agreed.

Chapter Twenty-Five

The first time Austin woke up, he couldn't open his eyes. He felt a veil lift from his consciousness, heard voices in the distant, but could feel nothing around him. Was he laying down? Was he dead?

"...a few more days..."

He did not recognize the voice at first. But he clung to the melodic sound. Even as someone else responded, their words blurring into nothing, he waited to hear that voice again.

"I'm just happy that he's..."

That he's what? Were they talking about him? Austin tried prying his eyes open but it only wore him down. The veil began to fall once more and the voice faded into nothing.

***

When he woke again, he could open his eyes this time. He didn't know where he was. He stared up at an ornate ceiling with white, intricate moulding and thought that this certainly was not his townhouse.

No one was speaking this time. Instead, he heard the soft hum of rain outdoors, casting the room in a soft shadow. With what little strength he had, he looked around, trying to get an understanding of his surroundings.

And then his eyes fell on her. She was asleep, a book laid across her lap and her head tilted towards. She snored softly, hair covering most of her face.

Austin tried to move, to reach out to her. She sat next to him, so close yet still so far. He tried to speak, to wake her. But he found himself going under once more and his eyes closed to the sight of her sleeping soundly beside him.

***

He thought that perhaps the next time would be the last time. Dipping in and out of consciousness was fast getting old. He heard voices that brought him from the brink of sleep many times but he was gone mere seconds after that he hardly considered those times, even though he remembered them. This time, however, Austin had enough strength to open his eyes again.

Lavender was the first thing he saw. She was not sitting next to him this time but standing by the window. It was raining again and she stared outside with a wistful expression on her face.

"It's been far too long," she said after a while.

Something moved in the left corner of the room. Austin recognized the person a beat after. It was Miss Alice.

"Keep your faith, Lav," she said softly, giving her friend a sad look. "I'm sure he will wake soon."

"But what if he doesn't, Alice?" Lavender asked. She wiped at her cheek. Austin realized that she was crying even though he could not see her tears. "What if I do not get the chance to tell him?"

Alice crossed over the room to her and enveloped Lavender in her arms. Lavender did not hesitate to bury her face into her friends shoulders.

"You will," Alice assured her.

Austin sighed softly and prayed that either woman heard. His eyes drifted closed on their own accord a second after, so he didn't know if they did. He realized suddenly that the same fear consumed him.

What if he didn't get to tell her either?

***

He might have been under for far too long. That was his first thought when he opened his eyes again, hopefully for the last time. The first thing he noticed was that he had far more strength this time. The heavy weight of exhaustion did not hang heavily behind his eyelids this time. He blinked up at the ceiling and tried wriggling his finger. It worked.

The next thing he did was look around the room, only to see with a bit of disappointment that it was empty. He'd hoped to see

Lavender sitting in the chair by his bed. Slowly, not wanting to push himself, Austin sat up.

Something tickled his neck. Austin reached up and realized that it was his hair. It had grown out quite a bit while he'd been sleeping. How long had that been? With one touch to his cheek, he realized that his beard was almost full grown as well. Had it been weeks since he'd last woken?

He didn't even want to entertain the thought. He recalled the look of despair on Lavender's face the last time he saw her and could only imagine the worry he had caused. All because of his stupid pride and his inability to handle his own emotions.

Slowly, Austin pushed the covers aside. He had no intention of sitting in bed and waiting for someone to see him awake. He swung his legs over the side of the bed and waited for the wave of dizziness. None came. He stood and waited again. Still nothing.

Only then did he realize that he was dressed in nothing but a white cotton shirt and a pair of breeches. He even felt clean. Clearly he had been taken care of while he'd been unconscious.

Austin slowly made his way to the door. With every step, he felt his strength returning and by the time he made it to the hallway, he was walking as if nothing had happened.

He didn't know where he was going. The surroundings were unfamiliar to him and there was no one in sight. He made random turns without giving it much thought, hoping it would take him to the staircase since he was clearly not on the first floor.

At last, he found it. Austin held on to the railing as he descended though he felt fine, not wanting to risk anything. He made it to the landing without encountering a soul but at this point, he knew where he was.

Latrice Manor's foyer.

Austin headed to where he knew the drawing room was. The place he remembered he'd last been, fighting unconsciousness until it came to claim him so quickly that he hadn't been given a chance to issue a warning. He remembered his eyes closing and a second before he slipped under, he heard a scream that he would never be able to forget.

He heard her voice before he entered. His entrance was quiet enough that the others in the room did not notice him. He saw Vincent first, then Miss Alice, then...

Lavender sat in the furthest corner of the room, her back to the door. She seemed to paying keen attention to her embroidery, her fingers moving so rapidly that it was a wonder she didn't hurt herself. She looked as beautiful as the last time he saw her, most of her hair draped over one shoulder and her bare feet tucked into the grooves of the armchair she was sitting in.

Miss Alice and Vincent had their heads bent together, facing Lavender, undoubtedly talking about her in hushed tones and worried expressions. They were so caught up in what they were saying that neither one of them noticed him standing there.

A few seconds went by as the uncomfortable silence in the room deepened. Austin felt a prickle of amusement as he cleared his throat.

All three heads turned to him. He heard Miss Alice gasp, saw Vincent come to a stand. But his attention remained on Lavender who dropped her embroidery, her jaw going slack at the sight of him.

"Austin?" she murmured, her voice so soft that he almost didn't hear her.

Austin drifted to the center of the room. He tugged on his shirt. "Please tell me that this is mine. Because if it isn't, I have a serious problem with—"

He didn't get to finish his words when Lavender launched herself at him. He'd watched her stand up, watched as she hurried over to him, but was wholly unprepared for her to jump into his arms considering the fact that he had just been bedridden for who knows how long.

He didn't care though. Her scent wrapped around him that he moved without thought as well, tightening his arms around her. He buried his face in her hair, quietly breathing her in, grounding himself in her presence. Austin forgot all about Vincent and Miss Alice, caring only about the small woman in his arms who clung to him as if she never wanted to let go.

"What are you doing out of bed, you madman?" Vincent asked, approaching them.

Only then did Lavender pull away. Austin did as well, albeit reluctantly. She put a foot of distance between them but she stared up at him as if she was looking at a ghost.

"I don't like staying in one place for too long," he explained. "I woke up and no one was there. I wanted to see who it was that nursed me back to health." He looked back at her, unable to stop himself from brushing her cheek with the back of his hand.

Tears were rapidly filling her eyes. "I can't believe that you...that you truly..." She bit her quivering lip as the tears spilled over.

In the corner of his eye, he saw Miss Alice take Vincent's arm. "Perhaps we should give them privacy," she whispered to him.

"You want me to leave her alone with him?" Vincent whispered back, sounding incredulous.

"Yes," Miss Alice said simply. And he supposed that was that. Vincent protested no longer and allowed her to lead him out of the room.

Once again he was alone with Lavender. Last time, he'd had so many things to say and could not find the strength to say them. Now none of those words came to his mind, even though he felt them deep within his heart.

"I'm so glad," she said at last, "that you are all right. I was afraid that...that you would never wake up."

"How long was I asleep for?"

"Two weeks."

She said it softly, those two words were all he needed to hear to know that she had been suffering this entire time.

"When you fell unconscious I thought that you might have—" She broke off, swallowing, clearly unable to say the words aloud. "But then the physician informed us that you had simply suffered from a concussion. He said that you would be in a deep sleep and that, if we were lucky, you would awake on your own. And if you weren't..."

"There's no need to think about that anymore." He couldn't hold back. He pulled her back into his arms and was relieved when she did not protest, slipping her arms around his waist. She laid her head against his chest and he wondered if she could hear the rapid pound of his heart.

"Thank you for waking up, Austin. I did not want to assume the worst but with every day that went by, I..."

"I understand. Thank you for nursing me back to health. You were the only reason I was able to." She looked up at him in confusion and he smiled a little. "You didn't know this but I did become conscious a few times. The first time I only heard your voice, the second time you were sleeping next to my bed, and the third time you were standing by the window with Miss Alice. There were others as well but they went by so quickly that I hardly remembered them."

"How hadn't I noticed?" she gasped.

"Let's just be happy that we're here now." He gently rested her head back against his chest. He could stay like this forever he knew.

"Austin." Lavender pulled away again. "I want to apologise. For Colin and all the problems he caused you. He told me what happened and had it not been for the way that he provoked you perhaps none of this would have happened."

Austin sighed. "I hate to come to the defence of that man but the fault does not rest solely with him. I pushed him as well. And I was the one who insisted that we fight rather than walk away. I deserve what came to me."

"No, you don't," she insisted in a firm tone. "It's my fault, truly. You felt the need to defend my honour and for that, I am truly sorry. I..." She stepped away from him, holding her head down. "I understand if you want to step away from this. I will convince my brother to compensate you for all that you've done for me so far and I will make sure that your renovations are complete. And you don't have to worry about helping me with—"

"Oh my! Lavender." Austin didn't like the distance she'd put between them. He wanted her close, her skin against his, at all times. "Surely you must know by now that I do not care about such things."

Lavender frowned at him. "But isn't that why you decided to marry me in the first place?"

"Yes, before I knew you. Before I fell in love with you."

"But you—" She broke off, blinking. "You what?"

The dumbfounded look on her face made him smile. Austin reached out and brushed her hair behind her ears, cupping her face in both hands. "I am hopelessly in love with you. I am the one who is sorry that I did not tell you sooner."

"Oh."

That seemed like all she could muster. For the first time, Austin felt a sliver of uncertainty. He hadn't at all considered the thought that she might not feel the same way. But everything everyone had ever said about him came rushing back over all those years into this single moment. The uncouth, brutish bastard might not be the kind of man she could love. He might not be the kind of man she would truly want to marry.

He wiped away the twinkle of fear from his face even as it began to set root in his chest. "Would you like to marry me, Lavender?" he asked softly. "Considering the person that I am, someone who will spend every day trying to be a man you can be proud to call yours, do you still want to share my name?"

Lavender blinked at him. And then, to his utter relief, he saw the familiar shade of humor in her eyes. "Is that all you have, my lord?" she asked in a teasing voice.

"Well..." Austin pretended to think. "I must also mention that I have a title, which others might consider to be a selling point."

She tilted her head back to laugh. The sound was music to his ears. Lavender slid into his arms, grinning up at him.

"I love you too, Austin. Every bit of you, especially that title of yours."

Austin chuckled. He leaned in to kiss her gentle on her lips but she tipped into the kiss, deepening it. It stirred all the things that had been simmering under the surface for so long. Now that the truth of his feelings were out there, he didn't care to hold back. He didn't think twice about the fact that it might be deemed improper if they were caught like this.

"Do you see why I did not want to leave them alone?" Vincent's voice sounded from behind.

Lavender gasped and pulled away, turning two shades of red.

Miss Alice giggled. "And that is exactly why I thought to pull you away."

Epilogue

Two Months Later

She didn't think she would see the day.

It was the truth, even though it had taken Lavender far too long to come to terms with it. Despite her plans, despite what she'd wanted for herself, despite her insistence and determination, a part of her didn't think the day would come where she would walk down the aisle and be happy about it.

Happiness was one thing. Nervousness, fear, trepidation—those emotions crowded her glee until she could do nothing to fight it. She sat as still as a stone, staring at her reflection, her nerves a jumbled mess.

"I think this would be nice," Alice was saying behind her. Vaguely, Lavender took note of her friend holding up a headdress adorned with blue and white wildflowers. Next to her, Betty nodded in approval, but Alice was already moving on to the next option. "Or this one! Or perhaps this?"

Lavender only listened with half an ear. She couldn't believe the day was finally here. Months of preparation led up to this beautiful, terrifying moment.

"What do you think, Lav?" Alice asked.

Lavender blinked. She turned a bit too slow, trying to focus on what she was meant to be looking at. Alice had gone a little overboard in preparing Lavender's accessories for her wedding day. Her bed was covered in floral headdresses of varying colors.

"Any one is fine," she said half-heartedly.

"You can't just choose any one," Alice chastised. "This is your special day. You must choose the perfect one."

Lavender pointed, knowing that she wasn't indicating to anything in particular. "That one then," she murmured.

Alice's brows knitted together. "Which?" she asked.

"The blue one,' Lavender answered. Her mind was already drifting to what would happen in mere hours. Was Austin already waiting for her in the gardens? What would he think when he saw her? Hopefully he wasn't already thinking that this was a mistake?

"Give us a moment, please," she heard Alice say. Without really seeing, Lavender watched as Betty nodded in understanding and retreated from the room.

Alone now, Alice sank onto the bed, facing her. "What is the matter, Lav?" she asked gently.

Lavender nearly shook her head. She almost told her that it was nothing but nerves. But this was more than just nerves. She was so eager for this that she was afraid. Afraid of losing something she never thought she would have.

"What if he decides he does not want this any more, Alice?" Lavender murmured.

Alice's expression softened. "Is this why you haven't said anything for some time now?"

"I was excited at first," Lavender explained. "But now I cannot help but overthink..."

"Don't," Alice said gently. "I have seen the way Lord Derby looks at you, Lav. And considering how he looks at everyone else, believe me when I say that it is quite a difference."

That brought a giggle to Lavender's lips. She'd continued dragging Austin from event to event these past two months and had gotten a lot of pleasure out of watching him interact with her peers. More than one of them came to her in private asking her if she was certain she wanted to marry someone so angry all the time.

"He loves you, Lavender. Anyone with eyes can see it."

"Do you think?"

"What do you feel for him?"

She couldn't put those feelings into words. Lavender blushed, suddenly shy at the thought of expressing it aloud.

Alice laughed, waving her hand dismissively. "Never mind, then. Your expression is all I needed to see. Everything will be fine, Lavender. Trust me. And you look absolutely lovely, if you were doubting that as well. Now," Alice stood, turning to the bed, "why don't you choose?"

Lavender laughed and settled on a headdress adorned with marigolds. Alice excitedly called Betty back in and the two of them seemed to take quite a lot of pleasure in fussing over Lavender. By the end of it, she wore a loosely-fitted muslin and lace cream-colored gown that went nicely with her headdress.

Some of the fear disappeared by the time she was ready to head down to the gardens. The renovations to Austin's townhouse had included refreshing the garden so she had thought it was the perfect place to have the ceremony, especially considering the fact that his estate was not yet ready. She needed only say those words and Austin had done what he needed to do—announcing the wedding banns at last, acquiring a special license, even indulging her in hosting an engagement ball at the house. Lavender asked and he'd done what she wanted without question, even if he didn't particularly like it. Perhaps he truly did love and adore her as much as Alice said.

Lavender smiled to herself, a little embarrassed that she had used her insecurities to doubt him. Austin had spent nearly every day showing her just how much he loved her and Lavender had done her best to do the same. Why would today of all days be different?

They made it to the first floor before Vincent came upon them. "Pardon me, Miss Alice," he said. "But may I steal my sister away for a moment."

Alice nodded. "But don't keep her for too long. The guests are waiting."

"Yes, yes, she won't allow it, I'm sure," Vincent said with a grin.

Alice returned the smile and stepped away, leaving them alone.

"Let's go to the drawing room," Vincent suggested. He took the lead and Lavender followed, saying nothing though curiosity nagged at her.

It had taken a little bit of time to convince Vincent of the love between Austin and her. He wouldn't deny her a thing, which was why he didn't dare to suggest ending the betrothal again, but his wariness of Austin had taken some time to deplete. But understandably so. After everything that had happened, Lavender knew that it would take some time for Vincent to trust Austin around her again.

But she doubted he would pull her away on the day of her wedding to voice his displeasure. Would he?

Lavender studied his face the moment they were behind closed doors. The pleasant expression he'd given Alice was gone, looking far more grim.

"What's the matter, Vincent?" she asked, her nervousness creeping back up her spine.

Vincent said nothing, pulling out a letter from behind his waistcoat. Wordlessly, he handed it to her.

Lavender's nervousness morphed into confusion when she saw that it was from the Countess of Lively. She glanced back up at her brother but he only stood there waiting for her to read.

The letter was…lengthy. It began rather politely—or as polite as Lady Lively could be—before she delved into paragraph after paragraph of rude statements, expressing how disappointed she was that she was not invited to the wedding.

By the end of it, Lavender was laughing. Vincent looked surprised. "Does it not bother you?" he asked.

"Bother me?" Lavender shook her head, refolding the letter. "Of course not. Lady Lively backed herself into the corner I wanted her to be in this whole time. I find it rather amusing that she did it on her own, after I have decided to leave my quest for revenge alone."

"But she was rather nasty in her letter. I thought you would have been upset by it. The only reason I showed it to you now is because I thought it might upset you if you were to learn of it afterward."

"I'm fine, Vincent. It's fine. I don't care anymore."

That shocked him. "It does not?"

Lavender shook her head, smiling. It felt nice saying aloud what she had been admitting to herself all along. "I was haunted by her. She hounded my every thought, my every action. But after finding love, Vincent, I realised that I have no more room in my heart for hate." She handed the letter back to him. "She does not matter anymore. Though it is quite amusing that she is this upset at the fact that she was not invited to the wedding of a mere sister of a merchant and a bastard earl."

Austin helped her, of course. He hadn't said as much in words. He was committed to helping her take her revenge, no matter what. But as the days went on, Lavender didn't care about making a perfect impression at each event and following every tiny detail of her plan. She didn't care about what Lady Lively was saying about her, or climbing her way to the top of the social ladder so that she could knock the queen off her throne. She only cared about spending time with the people she loved.

Vincent smiled at that, his eyes filling with pride. "There she is," he said. "Then what would you like for me to say in response?"

"Whatever you wish, Vincent. You needn't say anything at all, truly, though that may just upset her further."

"Silence it is." He approached, pulling her into an embrace without warning. "I'm proud of you, Lavender."

"Thank you. Now, may I go ahead? Alice may be sweet but she is quite terrifying when she's cross."

"I don't doubt it," Vincent chuckled. "Now that you are in such a good mood, perhaps I should show you the letter you received from your old friend, Colin."

Lavender was already shaking her head. Colin had sent her many letters over the past two months. And if they were ever in the same place at the same time, she would catch him staring at her from across the room, though he never dared to approach. They were yet to talk about what had happened between them but Lavender had still invited him to the wedding. It had only surprised her a little that he said he could not attend.

That was fine, though. She wasn't ready to face him just yet. Certainly not on a day like today.

"Perhaps tomorrow," she suggested. "Or perhaps after we return from our honeymoon."

Before Vincent could respond, there was a knock on the door. Alice poked her head in. "I do not mean to be rude," she said with an overly bright smile. "But your time is up, Mr. Latrice. I am here to steal her away."

"Very well, I know better than to fight for more time with my sister before she is passed into the hands of another," Vincent sighed. "I shall walk with you."

They left the drawing room and with every step Lavender took to the back of the house, the more her nerves came upon her again. She could hear the soft tune of a harp as they delved outdoors. It was a beautiful morning, a cloudless sky with a gentle breeze. To the back of the garden stood a small clearing and a gazebo where everyone was waiting.

Lavender saw him before he saw her. Austin stood under the gazebo with the priest, his hands clasped behind his back and that scowl on his face. The music grew louder and the very few guests they had invited turned to watch her approach. He didn't look until she'd already gotten a good look at him and had to catch her breath.

He was so handsome that she couldn't stop the smile that stretched across her face. Any remnants of the bruises from two months ago had faded almost completely, his clean-shaven state showing off his lovely, sharp jawline. Her heart fluttered when their eyes met and the scowl faded into something else, something that was only reserved for her. Lavender was hardly aware of the people around her, nor of Vincent walking her down the aisle. She only saw him, any anxious or fearful thought escaping her mind.

"God, you look..." He was at a loss for words. Austin ran his gaze down the length of her, then shook his head. "I am the luckiest man in London."

"And don't you forget it," she teased, earning a chuckle from him. He took both her hands in his.

"I thought you would have me waiting forever," he confessed in a whisper. "For a second, I thought that you might have changed your mind."

It touched her that he might have had the same doubts as her. "There is nowhere I would rather be but here," she murmured to him. "And nothing I would rather become but your wife."

His eyes slid away even as she saw the faintest tinge of pink on his cheeks. Confessing the depth of their feelings always made him shy, a sight that was endlessly adorable to her.

He didn't get the chance to respond when the priest cleared his throat, obviously wanting to get on with the ceremony. They faced him but Austin didn't let go of her hand. As the priest began reading from the Book of Common Prayer, Lavender half-listened, half-waited.

How could she truly focus when he was rubbing the back of her hand with his thumb like that? And sneaking her glances when the priest was looking in his book? How was anyone supposed to remember her vows—despite having practiced them many times over—when he stared so intently at her that it felt as if her entire being had been set on fire?

Lavender loved him. Truly, she loved this man. How could she show him the depth of her love when it felt as if she could hardly control it herself?

And then, at last, it came for them to seal their union with a kiss.

And seal it, they did.

Lavender stepped closer, lips quirking upwards at the flash of surprise in his eyes. Then she captured his lips. Reminiscent of their first kiss, she wanted to give as much as he did, to show him that she was his and his alone. She wanted him to know just how much she loved and yearned for him because she was beginning to think that no word known to man could show it well enough.

Austin must have forgotten that they had an audience. Or perhaps, more likely, he didn't care. He grasped the back of her head and leaned fully into the kiss, taking control with ease. Lavender wrapped her arms around his neck, clinging to him as he bent her into the kiss.

It must have lasted a second or two, but it felt like a lifetime and no time at all. When they came up for air, she realized that the others were applauding.

"That wasn't very ladylike of you, Lady Derby," Austin whispered in her ear.

"Good," she whispered back. "I didn't want it to be."

Austin's deep chuckle resonated throughout her, making goose pimples rise on her skin. "I love you."

That was enough to chase away any lingering doubt. Things might not have ended up the way she'd planned and for that, she could not be happier.

Extended Epilogue

Two Years Later

"You look quite pleased with yourself."

Lavender tilted her head towards him without looking. Austin loved it when she did that. Tilting her head close, taking a step towards him, turning her body slightly to face him. She didn't have to look at him. Her entire body language invited him into her space, showing him that he had her undivided attention even if her eyes remained on something else.

"Shouldn't I be?" she asked with a smile touching her lips. She sipped her wine, eyes scanning the crowd of guests filling their lavish ballroom. "Everyone seems to be enjoying themselves, don't you think?"

"Without a doubt." He came closer to the railing. They stood on a mezzanine overlooking the ballroom, behind them a door that led to a balcony under the night's stars. It had been Lavender's suggestion. After they returned from their honeymoon two years ago, they'd moved to the countryside manor despite the fact that the renovations were still underway. She'd made a passing remark that it would be lovely to have a mezzanine in the ballroom and Austin had instantly given orders to include it.

He couldn't doubt that he liked it as well. She had a natural gift for these things.

The sight of the full ballroom still instilled disbelief in Austin. He didn't think that so much could change in so little time. When they'd gotten married, there had been a bit of buzz about their union but nothing to turn too many heads. Yet, Lavender's natural introduction to the world of nobles had led to her instant popularity. She didn't have to try, didn't have to plan what she would wear or say. If they received an invitation to a ball or a soiree, she would always try to attend. And by the end of the night, she had nearly everyone in the palm of her hand.

Their popularity grew to such an extent that everyone vied to attend a ball thrown by the Countess of Derby. For those who did not receive an invitation, they would send a letter asking to for permission to attend. And Lavender, being who she was, would always accept.

Even the Countess of Lively was in attendance.

She did not beg for an invitation. But every time she was not asked to attend an event being hosted by the Earl and Countess of Derby, she ensured that everyone knew how displeased she was. Austin often wondered if she noticed how bitter she seemed as a result, marring her otherwise pristine reputation. But envy was a nasty drink and Lady Lively constantly looked as if she spoon-fed it to herself every morning.

Lavender saw it as well and decided to invite her now and again, out of pity. Right now, she stood near the center of the ballroom surrounded by her usual posse of lackeys and watching the current dancers with an upturned nose.

Austin shook his head at the sight. Lavender no longer cared about Lady Lively so he didn't either. He took a step closer to his wife, sliding his arm around her and not caring who saw.

"Do you think we can sneak away for a moment?" he whispered in her ear.

She rested her head on his shoulder, giggling. "I think a few people will notice if we were gone for too long."

"Ah, I see. Allow me to change my wording then. Do we care if our absence is noticed?"

Boldly, she turned to face him, eyes gleaming as she wrapped her arms around him. Their constant displays of affection was often a topic of discussion amongst others and, as usual, neither one of them cared.

"Now *that* I should think about." She made a show of thinking by rolling her eyes to the ceiling. "And the answer is an easy, no. I don't care."

Austin shared her conspiratorial grin as he slid his hand down to capture hers. He took the lead, pulling her behind him as they delved towards the staircase set to the left of the mezzanine. Austin intended to take her out into the gardens, which had quickly become Lavender's favorite place to be next to the library. Though it would not be under the warm sun, he was sure she would enjoy a nice evening walk.

The moment they arrived in the midst of the ball, they were approached by a gaggle of young ladies.

"My lady!" one of them gushed. "I did not get the chance to tell you how lovely you looked this evening!"

"Thank you, Lady Georgia," Lavender responded kindly. Her warm smile had the ladies coming closer, as if drawn in like a moth to a flame.

"May I ask how you managed to style your hair that way?" another one of them asked, eyes sparkling with excitement.

There were five of them and could not be any older than ten-and-seven. Austin wasn't certain any one of them had debuted as yet but their mothers had grown so fond of Lavender that they had no qualms allowing their daughters to attend this evening's ball. Austin didn't know any of their names, though their faces were a little familiar.

"Well, I will have to ask my lady's maid, Lady Hannah," Lavender responded with a laugh. She knew the girls very well. In fact, she was acquainted with everyone in attendance. Austin didn't know how she managed to do it.

He took a step back and watched as these girls hung onto every word Lavender said. She was always gentle and kind, jesting now and again. He wondered if she realized that she'd fulfilled her old plan. Not out of revenge but from simply being herself. Without intending to, Lavender had dethroned Lady Lively and everyone seemed to be aware of it except her.

After a while of admiring her, he decided he'd had enough of sharing her. "If you would excuse us, ladies," he said, stepping in. He placed his hand on the small of Lavender's back, already steering her away.

Lavender ushered apologies to girls as she was led away from them. She slapped Austin lightly on the chest. "That was rude," she chastised.

"I am known for being rude," he said simply. He kept his eyes on the goal, the terrace doors across the room. With everyone wanting to engage with the hostess, those doors felt too far away.

"And I suppose it is one of the things I love about you." She sighed as if it tired her.

After two years, Austin was beginning to think he would never get tired of hearing those words.

They were almost there. A few people tried to stop them as they went by. Even Vincent, who had been visiting them for the past week, tried to speak with Austin about business matters. Austin rightfully told him that they could speak about such matters another time and kept moving.

The doors were almost within reach. And then Lady Lively stepped into his path.

She was accompanied by Lady Anna, her constant shadow. Austin still didn't feel comfortable being near her, even though the marquess' daughter had married her own earl. He would never forget how her bold impropriety, disguised under gentle smiles and ladylike mannerisms, had caused a rift between Lavender and him.

Lavender didn't seem to mind the lady half as much. She smiled warmly at her and Lady Anna returned it, though it didn't touch her eyes.

Austin's attention was on Lady Lively though.

Bitterness and jealousy had aged her like nothing else could. Lady Lively, once the most popular lady in England, now had the reputation of a hateful lady who did nothing but gossip. Why others were only just realizing that was a mystery to Austin. But anything concerning Lady Lively no longer mattered to Lavender so he supposed it did not matter to him either.

Even so, he couldn't stop his guard from going on when the countess locked eyes with his wife.

"Lady Derby," Lady Lively began with a false, tight smile. "I have not gotten the chance to speak with you all evening. One would think that you were avoiding me."

"I have no reason to do such a thing," Lavender responded simply. "How do you do, Lady Lively?"

"I am well. Though I must say it is a little stuffy in here. Don't you think there are too many people, or perhaps you were hoping to make an impression by inviting half of England."

"If you are feeling confined, my lady, feel free to leave. I'm sure no one will mind."

Lady Lively's smile slipped. "If I dare to leave now, nearly half of these people will leave right behind me. Your ball will become quite a disaster if that were to happen, I'm afraid."

"If that is what you wish to believe, my lady, I can do nothing to stop you."

This time, Lady Lively barely managed to hold back her sneer. And Austin struggled to hold back his laughter.

He enjoyed standing back and listening to Lavender cut through the countess' hubris with firm politeness. He watched as she struggled to find something to say in response.

Lady Anna attempted to come to her rescue by saying, "My lord, I must say that I find your art pieces quite tasteful. May I enquire about the artists?"

The Austin before Lavender would have told her to leave him be, or simply ignored her altogether. The man he had become attempted to be polite instead. "I do not recall the name of the artist," he admitted. "They were commissioned by my late father a long time ago."

"How sad. I would love to have that person paint my own portrait. I have been looking for some time now." Lady Anna pointed to the painting hung on the north wall. "Even from here, I can tell that the lady in the painting was a beauty. The brushstrokes are so subtle that it is as if she is staring right at me."

Austin didn't bother to hold back his smile. He looked at the painting in question, meeting the eyes of familiar blue ones. He could almost feel Lavender's pleasure as she said, "Yes, I must agree, my lady. I thought there would be no other painting more fit to be hung in one of the most important rooms in our manor."

"Who is she, if I might ask?"

"A very important person to me," Austin answered. He didn't need to say any more than that. Though he couldn't help but wonder what these ladies would say if they knew they spoke highly of his father's mistress, a mere maid.

Lavender had insisted that they bring the painting with them to the estate, after spending nearly an entire day rummaging through his father's old things. And it hadn't taken much convincing for him to hang it in the ballroom. He knew better than to reveal who she truly was. But it seemed as if no one cared to ask, perhaps assuming that she was simply another family member.

"If you would forgive us, ladies," Lavender spoke up. "I hope you two enjoy the rest of your evening."

She stepped away without giving either one of them the chance to respond. Austin was happy to follow. Finally, they made it all the way to the gardens without being stopped again.

Silence settled over them. Austin slung his arm around her shoulders, pulling her close. Lavender wrapped her arm around his waist and rested her head on his shoulder. They said nothing as they delved down a quiet path lit with moonlight.

"Do you think they will leave?" he asked after a long while.

"I do not care what they do," Lavender said. "Honestly, I would not mind if everyone left. I want to be alone with my husband."

"Are we not alone right now?" he asked with a chuckle.

She shook her head. He glanced down, heart warming at her small pout. "Not alone enough. Even now I can hear the voices of others walking about our garden."

"I thought you loved throwing balls."

"I do, I do. But I like having intimate alone time with you as well. Especially when I wish to tell you a secret I have been keeping for weeks now."

Austin paused, frowning down at her. "A secret," he echoed.

Lavender's grin was broad. "Yes, and I must say that I nearly gave in and told you many times already."

Austin only stared at her. When it became clear that she had nothing else to say, he asked, "Well? What is it?"

She was teasing him, dangling this secret over his head. "Patience, my love. Before I say it, I must say that I considered making a toast. But then I thought that I should tell you first before revealing it to others."

"And what exactly would you be revealing?"

Lavender giggled. She took his hand and placed it on her stomach. Austin's eyes went wide. He didn't know how he hadn't noticed before. He had taken note of the fact that she was eating far more, and seemed to have restless nights at times. But he hadn't thought much about it.

Now he understood.

"Are you serious?" he whispered, almost afraid to hear the response.

Lavender nodded. Her eyes were already swimming with tears. "The physician finally confirmed it. And believe me when I say that it has been quite difficult hiding it from you. But I did not want to say anything that might get your hopes up."

"You're with child?" Austin asked dumbly.

Lavender nodded, wiping her tears. "I am. It's finally happened, Austin. We're going to have a chi—"

She didn't get the chance to finish before he picked her off the ground, spinning her around. Her laughter echoed around him.

"We're going to have a child!" he laughed, setting her back on her feet. He kissed her because he was so happy. He kissed her again because he loved her and would love this child just as much. He kissed her yet again as a silent promise that he would everything in his power to be a great father as he tried to be a great husband.

Lavender kissed him back as if she understood all the words he didn't have to say. She framed his face in her hands. "I love you, Austin."

"I love you too, Lav."

When their lips met again, Austin never wanted to pull away. Even though he was looking forward to their future, to raising the family they had been trying to have for years.

For right now, this moment, he wanted this kiss to last forever.

The End

Printed in Great Britain
by Amazon